The Well of Life

NAWAL EL SAADAWI

The Well of Life
and
The Thread

TWO SHORT NOVELS

Translated from the Arabic by Sherif Hetata

LONDON TORONTO

First published in Great Britain 1993
by Lime Tree
an imprint of Reed Consumer Books Ltd
Michelin House, 81 Fulham Road, London SW3 6RB
and Auckland, Melbourne, Singapore and Toronto

A CIP catalogue record for this book
is available from the British Library
ISBN 0 413 45431 2

Printed and bound in Great Britain
by St Edmundsbury Press, Bury St Edmunds, Suffolk

PJ 7862 .A3 W4 1993

The Well of Life

The ambulance had picked up the wounded man from a spot near the river and was speeding through the region of Al Aghuar when we spotted a ghostly apparition chasing behind us. It was as though the earth had split open suddenly to let it through.

After a short moment we realized it was a woman running after the car. I asked the driver to stop. As soon as the ambulance came to a halt she rushed up to it, looked eagerly into the face of the wounded man, and started to turn his feet and hands over between her fingers. She was so completely engrossed in what she was doing that she paid no attention to us, and said not a single word. The young militant who had accompanied the wounded man gently pushed her aside. I was on the verge of asking her what she was looking for, but the driver said, with a note of sadness in his voice: 'She neither hears what people say, nor does she answer them when they speak to her. During the day we often see her wandering about between the tents, while all the time looking around her, and, when night falls, she stretches her body out on the bank of the river. As soon as she catches sight of a man who looks as though he has been wounded, or sees his body being pulled out of the river, she jumps to her feet and runs up to where he is, stares into his face with searching eyes and examines his hands and feet carefully as though she is looking for someone she knows.'

I saw this woman many times during the period I spent in El Salt. Sometimes I would glimpse her running in the wake of an ambulance car. At other times she would be kneeling on the ground, half hidden between the rocks that covered the area in many parts, digging with her hands in the ground, or sitting with her gaze fixed on the horizon.

I had never had a chance to look into her eyes, but one day she was wandering around between the tents when I came face to face with her. She lifted her face and looked at me. I saw two enormous eyes sinking deep into their sockets, their surface covered by what looked like a thin film, like tears shed over many years which had dried. And under her left eyebrow was a small scar.

As soon as I took over my work in the clinic located in El Salt I sent a letter to Cairo in which I expressed a wish to prolong my stay. But the answer that came back from the authorities was negative, and was followed by the speedy despatch of another doctor to replace me. I am a woman and a woman doctor was not supposed to work in El Salt until the race of men doctors had disappeared off the face of the earth.

I returned to Cairo without finding out what became of this woman. I tried to write something about my mission to Jordan but every time I held the pen between my fingers her face would appear before me. I could see her enormous eyes look at me from their deep sockets, their surface covered by that film made by tears drying over the years, and the scar showing just under her left eyebrow.

Her thin, elongated body was stretched out on the riverbank. She lay there resting as though after a long journey covered on foot, or perhaps exhausted from a unending vigil in which she had never closed her eyes. Her lids were closed as though she were deep in sleep. In fact she was neither asleep nor awake. She was perhaps in a state of unconsciousness but different to the usual one in which people are not aware, nor can feel what is going on around them. The state she was in is extremely rare. It was a state where a human being can lose all sensation completely, and yet maintain a capacity to feel not only in a normal way, but with a sensitivity increased tenfold, and which permits the person to feel the lightest touch, hear what is inaudible, smell the faintest odour in the air and see movement before one can say it is there.

She did not know what had endowed her with this remarkable capacity for sensing things, for feeling, and although she did not know, yet she would be there for hours stretched out on the riverbank. If a fish happened to glide through the water she spotted it. If a leaf fell from a tree she could hear it as it settled lightly on the ground. If the faintest smell was wafted in the air she could sniff its scent. It might come from the smoke of a cigarette butt, or a car approaching in the distance, or the breathing of someone hiding behind the rocks. Her ears would tremble, her nostrils dilate and her big, black eyes would grow even bigger.

If she realized that there was nothing going on she would close her eyes again, her ears would become still and her nostrils would narrow to their normal size. Seeing her lying stretched out like that, one could imagine she was doing nothing, but this was not true. She was doing something, or, to be more precise, things were happening even if they were not willed by her. They were happening as they always had, repeating themselves in the same way, at certain times, in certain places and one after the other in exactly the same order. It was like a tape turning round and round on a reel, on which the days of her life followed one after the other, each day falling into its slot with nothing changing.

Her life did not begin with the day on which she was born, as is usually the case. In fact it started quite a time before that when she was still a small body in her mother's belly, just an embryo, yet capable of feeling and seeing and perhaps even smelling. Since darkness surrounded her day and night, there was nothing much to see apart from the darkness itself. Sometimes a faint ray of light would come to her from lower down, from a place she could not describe. Her eyes were still closed, and the optic nerve had not emerged, yet she could sense the light like a shadow over the lids of her inexistent eyes.

There was nothing to smell except for that smell which used to reach her nose at different times. She had no nose at the time. It was just a hole which had still to become a hole, so that her nose could develop around it.

However, that she could feel was something she had no doubt about. To her it was so clear and definite that it left no room for doubt. It was not what we usually call feeling, but something else, a minute sense of awareness, of certain things going on around her. She was only a piece of flesh, but this flesh was alive, not dead. Besides, it was flesh, not fat, and was made of very sensitive cells, all of which, or at least most of which, were of the type we call nerve cells. They kept dividing and dividing into hundreds and thousands and millions, or even millions of millions, of cells.

She knew she was inside her mother's belly, but felt she would not remain inside for all time. Inside her mother's belly was a long cord which crossed over and wound itself around her neck. At this stage she did not really have a neck, yet it seemed to wind around it and almost choke her, but she managed to avoid being suffocated. Every time the cord tried to strangle her she would shrink, become smaller and smaller, and her cells would press themselves up against one another. It was thus that she was able to save her skin, as people say. Yet she had no skin to speak of, since the time had not come for it to develop. She did not have a head, or a chest, or a belly. She was still a small body rolled up around itself with, like everything else, a front part and a back part. She knew the front part would become her head, and the back part would become something else. However, she did not know what her back should be called. It was something with a complicated name, not simple at all like the part called head. In fact it was so complicated that she might not have been able to pronounce it even if she knew.

Everything around her was dark and cool, conducive to a feeling of security, and to continued growth, except for something which used to occur from time to time. If only she could anticipate it, be ready for it when it came! But it used to happen so suddenly, with no fixed time or definite sequence of events. Usually at the beginning there would be strange voices. It could be the voice of her mother she was hearing since it seemed to be located somewhere high up. She could not distinguish words, since there were no words, only a kind of muttering, or growling, or sobbing. The sobbing would become violent and deep. Her mother's body would tremble and shake in a terrible way; she had to bury her delicate nailless fingers into the wall on which she lay to avoid herself from falling into the well which was below her some distance away. It was not really a well. In a well the water is motionless, but here it was like a whirlpool in the sea. It went round and round, all the time getting narrower and narrower, until its centre became a dark hole where death seemed to lie in wait.

She used to crouch, holding on to the wall, pressing herself up against it. She was like a louse sticking to the scalp of a head covered with hair. She held her breath, and under her sealed lids her frightened eyes would run here and there as she waited for that thing to pass through the hole, waiting for the long sharp blade that glittered in the dark to move up from below. Like a burning, fiendish eye, its shining, pointed tip crept up towards her. She would pull in her limbs, wedge herself in a deep furrow lining the humid, sticky wall, and wait trembling with fear. The pointed, shining tip skirted around her with quick movements like a blind monster scenting its prey. Sometimes its sharp edge hit against her flesh from below. Her cells would fold up quickly to shelter her wound and stop the blood from flowing.

*

So when Ain was born it was against her mother's will.*
And from the day when she was born there was that
scar, that old wound under her left eyebrow. Nobody
ever told her how long it had taken for her to be born,
whether it happened all of a sudden, in a minute, or
whether it was gradual, a long, slow moment lasting all
night. Her mother was in the tent, lying on the ground.
All around was a complete silence broken only by the
sound of a breeze gently shaking the wall of the tent, by
the regular, quiet snores of the father interrupted every
now and then as he turned over, only to resume their
monotonous rhythm like the monotonous tick of a clock
on the wall.

Suddenly the snoring stopped. There was the
sound of a quiet moan. The father opened his eyes,
then lifted his head to look at his wife. She was sleeping
on her side at the other end of the tent. Her big,
swollen belly protruded in front, separated from him
only by the brick they had put between them on the
floor. He closed his eyes again but another moan, louder
than the first, made him sit up. Now she was making
subdued, regular moaning noises. He raised his half-
closed eyes and looked at the narrow strip of sky
showing through the open slit of the tent. The night
was still dark. She was sure to give birth to the child
sometime after midnight. Did not women always give
birth to their children after midnight? He stretched out

* *Ain* in Arabic means 'eye' or 'well'.

his arm and quietly pulled off the only blanket covering her body. She was a woman, created to give birth to children and to suffer pain. He had done what was required of him and could resume his slumber outside the tent in the open.

The mother opened her eyes. They lay sunken deep in their sockets, large, luminous. All she could glimpse was a faint light traversing the slit in the door. The wind began to blow strongly, flapping the walls of the tent more and more. The pain crept round from her belly to her back, and began to shoot down her back like a sharp knife cutting through her flesh. She pushed the tail of her long robe beween her lips and clenched it with her teeth to stifle her screams and prevent her teeth from biting her tongue. Then she wound her arms around the two poles as though throwing the burden of her pain on to them.

Everything started to rise to a peak of violence, like a storm bursting out. The wind whipped the tent, making it flap with a resounding noise. The tent poles heaved and shook under the weight of her suffering body, the pain wracked and wrenched her in wave after wave, mounting to a summit, where it becomes no pain, or almost so.

She opened her eyes. Perhaps they were already open, yet it seemed to her that she had never opened them before. For the first time she was seeing the things around her. The ground on the other side of the tent was covered by a thin, worn blanket from under which protruded five small heads covered in long hair. She looked down between her thighs. The small, naked body had fallen face downwards, and was squirming like a worm, its bottom up in the air. She stretched out her hand instinctively and turned the child over on its back. Her big eyes moved deep in their sockets to follow the turning movement of the child's body and then settled on the narrow slit below the small, smooth belly. Her lids fell over her eyes, hiding them completely. Everything in front of her went pitch dark. Now it was a different pain which split her back into halves and shot down to the lower part of her belly and between her thighs, as though arising from a deep wound. Clots of cold blood welled up from her in an unceasing flow. She turned heavily over on one side, almost crushing the small, smooth body which lay underneath her. But from an early age Ain had learnt how to ward off death. She struggled and kicked until she managed to open a way for herself, sliding her small, smooth body out from between her mother's thighs.

Ain could not remember when it was that she had started to see things, to recognize the features which characterized different objects. Her eyes were always open, but at the beginning all she could distinguish were big, amorphous masses which moved here and there. She could recognize her mother by her loud voice and the smell of her milk. She would climb over her legs and arms, bury her face in the opening of her robe and search for her breast. Her greedy lips went over the emaciated breast, looking for the black nipple. Once they had found it her toothless gums would clench themselves around it and hang on desperately. Each time she longed to hold on until her hunger was appeased but the milk in the breast always dried up early; and her mother would pull her away from the nipple with an abrupt movement before she had a chance to be fed.

She would cry for a while and kick the air with her legs, but nobody seemed to hear her, so she stopped crying and started to stare around at things. Above her she could glimpse a black, cone-shaped wall which rose up but did not meet, leaving an open space. Her big, black eyes would fasten themselves on a slit in the wall from which the light came in. She wanted to look out through the slit, so she rested her hand on the wall of the tent for support and tried to stand on her feet. But the wall gave way under the pressure and she fell back on the ground where she was sitting. Meanwhile, the slit in the wall had grown a little wider and she was able to see her mother's face for the first time. She might have seen it before but now it was much clearer, despite the thick smoke which filled the air in the tent. She was able to glimpse huge, black eyes lying deep in their sockets, her big, pointed nose, and the thin, dry lips tightly closed over her mouth, opening now and then to let through angry noises, or strange mutterings. Then her big, white teeth would show and right in the middle of her mouth was one red tooth.

She did not know what were the clouds of smoke which almost hid her mother's face. She crawled on all fours towards her, gripped the tail end of her long robe, half lifted herself from the ground and tried to climb up by holding on to her legs. What she really hoped for was that her mother would bend down and lift her up in her arms. Then she would be able to find out about the smoke which kept hiding her mother's face from her. But her mother took no notice of her. She tried again and again but only to be rewarded with an angry kick, and her mother's angry voice cursing the day she was born.

But Ain would not give up. She moved away for a while, then came back to make another attempt. This time her mother kicked her even harder, but she insisted even more and did not let go until her mother lifted her up and permitted her to look into the pot. When the lid was taken off she felt a heat so strong that it burnt her face.

Each time she would insist. All she really wanted was simply this act of climbing up to her mother. So once her mother had exhausted all the kicks and curses she was capable of, and once she herself had used up all the obstinacy she could muster, her initial desire to discover the source of the smoke would give way to something new, to a desire which was much more pressing, a desire to triumph over her mother, to make her yield to her. She did not yet understand what 'to triumph' really meant. All she knew was that her mother's features would fall into an expression of sad resignation before her long arms stretched out to lift her up. Once her small body, wet with tears and sweat, had settled on her mother's broad chest, her muscles lost their tenseness and she let her body relax. She would be seized with a thrill of pleasure so strong, so fierce, that it seemed to be what she had really been seeking for right from the beginning. She would lay her small head on her mother's shoulder, and immediately all desire to stare into the pot was gone.

All this did not last very long. Soon she would be back on the ground, crawling on all fours, looking for something else to get a hold on. The tap looked to her like a small bird with a head and a tail. Her tiny hand groped through the air and curled its fingers around the neck. Suddenly a thin stream of water burst out from the hole in its tip. Another child would probably have chuckled or even screamed with laughter but not her. She knew how to clap her hand over her mouth and close her lips tightly together so that not a sound came out of them to alert her mother. She stretched out her hands to the water, and soon her arms and legs were all wet. She liked the feel of cold water on her body, so she put her head too under the tap, letting the water drip over her hair and neck.

Whenever her mother noticed that suddenly every-thing was quiet around her, she immediately guessed that Ain was engaged in some mischief. She could be playing with the pots and pans and utensils piled up in one corner of the tent, or she might have crawled to the stream of dirty water and be moulding the mud into cakes, or had perhaps opened the tap and might be emptying all the water in the earthenware jar.

Her mother soon discovered her sitting somewhere, all wet from top to bottom, her hair plastered on her head, her clothes sticking to her body, her feet swimming in a pool of mud and water. At that particular moment when her mother appeared she would be frightened, but she had lived with fear even before she was born and had learnt to overcome it if threatened by danger. Her cells were trained to block pain and to close wounds. If her mother beat her, or pinched her, she would swallow her tears and lick the skin where she had been hurt, so that the pain lasted no more than a few seconds.

Her mother would pull off the dirty wet clothes from her body as though she were skinning a rabbit. If her small arm happened to be caught or twisted in the narrow sleeve, she closed her lips tight to hold back the screams, for when her mother's anger mounted up she knew how to let the tears flow down her cheeks in silence. These tears were not the tears of pain. Her body had learnt how to swallow the pain and the tears which came with it deep down into her guts. These were tears of sadness, a sadness which showed through in a certain look and made the features of her mother's face relax into a kind of calm, made the touch of her hands more gentle, and the look in her eyes more soft, made her move closer to her and kiss her cheek quickly. A moment later, however, her mother's lips contracted, her face pulled back as though she wanted to suppress a strong yearning within her.

If we can call this a kiss, this is the first time Ain was kissed by her mother. In fact it was not a kiss, only a brief encounter no sooner begun than ended. It was perhaps not even an encounter, for her mother's lips were separated from her cheek by a small distance, fine as a hair but still enough to prevent a real encounter.

Yet though it was not a kiss, nor an encounter, it was still enough to make the heart under Ain's thin, tender ribs flutter with joy, to make her eyes shine with love when she looked at her mother. Now she was able to see the black shadow under the lashes around her mother's eyes. So she threw herself into her arms, buried her head into her mother's chest, sniffed the smell of breast milk landed down from long ago, took her nipple between her lips and sucked on the wasted breast. But her mother quickly shoved her away and sat her down amidst her sisters on the ground around the *tableya*.*

The *tableya* was the first place where she became

* *Tableya* – a low table for eating used by peasants.

acquainted with the other members of her family. Her father sat at its head, and her mother sat beside him. In front of her father lay a big dish. He ate from it and so did her mother. She and her sisters – there were five of them – sat on the other side of the *tableya*. In front of them was one dish from which they all ate together. The meal always took place in complete silence except for the loud sips of her father, or the gnashing of his teeth on a piece of bone. She lifted her eyes to his face and looked at his features. She had looked at them often before but this was the first time she was really seeing them. Somehow they did not seem to be familiar, the narrow slit eyes and the lids devoid of lashes, the wide forehead over which the sweat ran down, the thick, coarse nose below which grew long, black whiskers.

She forgot herself as she sat gazing into her father's face, and did not realize that meanwhile fifty small, emaciated fingers were dipping into the plate to snatch what was in it. When she came to herself and looked around with questioning eyes at her sisters, their faces all remained innocent-looking and strangely silent, for the plate was now empty.

As time went by she began to see things more clearly. It was as though the unchanging mist which seemed to envelope everything, or the white cloud which covered her eyes, had gone for ever. The first thing she tried to see was her own face. She had seen it many times before reflected in the surface of the stream, yet she was not familiar with its features so she tottered on her thin legs until she came to the stream, sat on its edge and gazed into the surface of its water. Two big eyes looked out at her. They resembled her mother's eyes. She stared fixedly into them. She was trying to find out how they looked exactly, for they looked strange to her and she wanted to get used to them. The more she looked at them the stranger they seemed to her, as though they were the eyes of another girl. This made her afraid of the stream, and of its water. It was not the exact feeling we mean when we use the word 'fear', and which makes you keep your distance, but rather a deep feeling of estrangement from herself. But parallel to this she developed an even stronger feeling, an urge to rid herself of this sense of estrangement. She approached her face right up to the surface and looked into her eyes so closely that her nose almost touched the water. Each time the feeling of estrangement seized hold of her she whispered to herself, 'This is me.' Sometimes she would be convinced and reassured, but at other times this odd feeling would be like a cold sheet of glass lying between her and the image of herself she could see.

These thoughts did not occupy her too much. There were many other things around her waiting to be discovered. When she stumbled on something new it always seemed to her that she had seen it before, known it before.

What was new was not new. A discovery was no discovery. It was as though she had lived her life before, and here she was living it again for the second or the third or perhaps the fourth time, so that now she could tell exactly what was going to happen tomorrow, or the day after. But this feeling lasted only a split second or perhaps even less. It was so quick and so short that it seemed as though she had not experienced it at all, as though it were some kind of illusion, a figment of her imagination.

She had nothing in particular to occupy herself with. She would sit out alone in the open. Her big, black eyes would keep circling around her. She was not looking for anything in particular, and yet one would have thought that she was. Sometimes she would dig in the earth with her thin fingers and turn the stones over between her hands. At other times she unearthed a beetle or a cockroach and kept turning it over on its belly, or its back. When she noticed the bulging eyes staring at her in abject humiliation, her body would be seized with a shivering, but she continued to squat where she was, holding her prey in her hands, pulling out a thin leg with its jarred edge, or tracing the line between the chest and the abdomen divided into segments.

Occasionally she played with the other children, joining in their competitions to see who could run faster, or jump further. When she jumped her naked thighs were often exposed, and she could see the scornful look in the eyes of the boys, and the way they gathered around whispering and laughing and shouting out rude, vulgar things. One, or even several of the boys might even run after the girls to hit them on their buttocks or breasts intentionally. The girls scattered in fright and were quickly swallowed up into the tents.

Ain was never frightened, nor did she run away. She gathered up stones and threw them at the boys. As soon as her hands were emptied of stones, she would pick up some more and throw them at the boys, on and on like that as though she would never stop, were it not for a huge hand that would come out of the tent, grasp her shoulder, and pull her in out of sight.

The tent was almost empty, for there was nothing much inside. Over the black, conical wall there was no roof. The worn blankets were piled up forlornly in a corner. Her five sisters slept huddled up against each other in a huge dark mass which had five heads and ten eyes. Ain had now started to pick up her sisters' names. The eldest one was Ba'a, the second Tha'a, the third Fa'a followed by Seen, then Sheen.* Her mother always got mixed up when she called out their names. When she wanted to call Ba'a she called out to Tha'a instead, and when she wanted to call Tha'a she pronounced Fa'a's name

---

* All letters of the Arabic alphabet. The author probably wants to say that they had no real identity, that they were not considered of any human value.

instead, and when she needed Sheen she would say Seen. Sometimes she called out all the five names one after the other before she finally pronounced the one she wanted. However, when she needed Ain she never made a mistake in her name, perhaps because Ain's name was very different from the others', or because on her face or body there were distinct markings such as the old scar under her left eyebrow. Or maybe it was that special look in her big, black eyes. It might have been just anything but the fact is that her mother never mistook her for any of her sisters.

Ain herself did not think that there was anything special about her. She was just another girl like her sisters. The fact of being a girl was not yet a part of her consciousness. She had heard of it through words and, like all things heard, it was subject to doubt. She had heard many things which were said to be true only to find out later that they were not. She wondered how she could find out whether she was a girl or not. She did not know of any way to do it. One day she hid herself behind the tent and pulled down her torn, dirty knickers and started to examine the part of her body which lay between her thighs. Her breath was coming in quick gasps and her heart was beating, but when her eyes settled on the narrow slit between her thighs, her breathing became more calm and her heartbeat slower. A feeling of something cold and heavy replaced the usual lightness of her body.

From that day onwards her past life started to appear to her in a different light. Words she had heard from her mother and not understood echoed once more in her ears, but now they had a meaning. The look she had seen in her father's eyes so often, now kept coming back, and now it was clear to her. Now she could explain it. The movements she had noticed at different times, and in different places, now had a new significance.

She came out from behind the tent, dragging a heavy body as though she were carrying a new burden. Her feet took her to the stream, impelled by a will of their own. She did not know where she was heading. She stopped at its edge and looked down under her feet. In the water she could see a reflection, a tall woman with two breasts, and two buttocks protruding. It was as though her breasts and her buttocks had grown in secret. Her femaleness, refused and unaccepted by everything around her, had decided to develop in hiding, to grow more than it needed, to store within itself surplus cells and so protect itself against the accidents she might have in the future.

Ain could not understand many of the things going on around her. Her sisters were disappearing from the tent one after the other. Each time she would hear strange whispers from behind the wall of the tent, and the sound of her father's hoarse voice talking to other men. It was not a real conversation but a series of sharp, direct questions which elicited answers formulated in figures and numbers. Then would begin a slow bargaining expressed mostly in muttering sounds. Her eyes travelled over the contents of the tent trying to find out what it was exactly that could be sold. Suddenly the voices would cease and her father would appear in the door of the tent calling out to one of his daughters. Her five sisters squatted in their usual corner, huddling up close to one another, like frightened chickens. A strong hand would creep out to grasp one of them by an arm or a leg, like a chicken being pulled out from a crowded wicker coop by the trader.

When the fifth sister disappeared, Ain began to wait for her turn. She did not know when it would come, but she was sure it would come sooner or later. She would wake up in the morning and put on the only robe she had. It had belonged to one of her sisters, was old and worn and black, covering her arms and legs, and tight over her chest and belly like a shroud wrapped around a body in a coffin. She would sit there waiting. Whenever she heard her father's voice her body would shiver. The moment it broke off she would jump to her feet, imagining all the time that he would appear the next moment, that her name would ring out, that her moment had come and that she had to make herself ready for it.

Often the voice she heard was not his, and he would not appear. All she could do then was to go back to her corner and resume her waiting. Her ears became sensitive to any sound, even if it was not the sound of her father's voice. Her eyes became sensitive to any shadow which approached the door of the tent. During the hot summer days, the sweat would pour from her body, her clothes would stick to her skin, and the air around her would seem to close in and suffocate her. She would stretch out her legs, close her eyes, and begin to fall asleep; but a moment later she started from her sleep and sat up with her eyes wide open. It was true that the important things did not happen in summer, especially in the middle of the day. Maybe none of her sisters' names had rung out in the still air, nor had her father ever appeared when the sun was still high in the sky above their heads, yet when the time came it came. Anything could happen. Perhaps at this very moment he would appear to call out her name in his hoarse voice.

The only thing she knew was that she was waiting for her turn. But what that meant, exactly, she did not know. Nevertheless, she waited. She had nothing else to do except wait, so waiting became her life. Nothing else to do except put on her black robe, sit in the corner, and wait. She no longer expected her father to come, and her name to ring out in the silence, since her father had not appeared nor had her name rung out before. In fact she now felt that the day when her name would ring out would never come. And yet she waited. It was like waiting for death and yet feeling that one would never die.

But the day came when her name echoed in the air. She was squatting in her usual corner. Her thighs were hurting terribly and her lids, heavy with sleep, were falling over her eyes, but she was making an effort to hold up the muscles of her face and keep them open. It was then that she heard her name called. She jumped to her feet, her heart beating with a feeling almost of happiness. But it was not that ordinary happiness, the one people are accustomed to feel, but something else, a feeling of salvation, of deliverance. She was being rid of this waiting. Her body felt light, her feet barely touched the ground on which she walked. They flew her to the door of the tent, almost leaving her father behind. She had no idea of what might be waiting for her outside. Yet she was seized by an overwhelming desire to throw herself into this encounter, were it death itself.

However, death was not what was waiting for her outside. It was something else, which could be worse than death. For death is, after all, no more than the fact of dying. All human beings are familiar with it, and all of them know it is their fate to die. But why should she be chosen, of all people, to live with the creature she saw standing before her? She could use no other description for him than that of 'creature', for he was not a human being, neither a young man nor an old man, neither a woman nor a man. She did not know what he was, exactly. Were it not for the words that came out of his mouth, were it not that he walked on two feet, she would have thought that he belonged to another species, a species she had never seen before.

He used to crawl towards her in the dark where she lay asleep and begin to pull off her clothes. The night was pitch black and she could not see anything but she kept her eyelids tightly closed. His breathing rent the silence of the night. It was not really a breathing but a series of wheezing gasps, cut through by bouts of coughing which sounded like a shrill whistle, as though the air flowed into his chest in one huge gulp and was then expelled slowly through a tiny hole. His hand felt over her body like a soft, heavy paw. She could not tell whether it was his hand or his foot but, whatever it was, it was always soft, amorphous and damp with sweat.

During the day he lay on his back in the tent. When he thought of getting up he extracted two wasted, bow legs with a shaking movement from under the blankets, and called out to her in a shrill complaint much like a dog howling. She would get hold of his foot and try to push it into his shoe, but his foot would shake and bend under the pressure. She could hear him rasp in angry tones, cursing her father and her mother. She repeated her attempt over and over again but each time his foot failed to enter the shoe. She tried to hold it with both hands but it slipped out time and time again, and lay there trembling and helpless on the ground. Losing his patience, he would suddenly kick her away, but a moment later he would call her back and start all over again.

When at last he succeeded in getting both feet into the shoes, he stood up and took a few paces. She did not think he was capable of walking but he walked. Of course he did not walk fast. It was more like a crawl in which he shifted from one corner of the tent to the other. If he spent some time outside he always came in gasping, coughing and cursing at the top of his shrill voice.

She could have gone on like this for the rest of her life. She knew no other way of living except the one that consisted of eating, drinking, sleeping and succeeding, after a few kicks and curses from him, in pushing her husband's miserable foot into his shoe. The kicks were not painful. They were the kicks of an ailing and impotent foot, and the curses did not matter since they were directed against her father and mother and not against her. Sometimes she would be seized by a strange, indefinable feeling, by an obscure sensation perceived by her body only. It was as though she were unable suddenly to breathe. Two powerful hands were throttling her around the neck. She would leap to her feet, open her mouth as wide as she could and gulp in the air; or she might just let out a muffled scream of fear. After a while, the feeling of suffocation would subside. Her breathing would become quiet and steady again. A feeling almost like a sudden joy would take hold of her.

She was happy not to have suffocated, happy to be still alive.

Ain might have continued to go on with her life in this way were it not for the woman. She did not know who this woman was. All she knew about her was that she lived in a neighbouring house. By 'neighbouring' she did not mean that it was the dwelling right next to hers. In fact it was quite far and could have been separated from her by many tents and houses, and even by a lake or a stream. It might even have been situated in another area. But in any case it was not so far away that she could not see it.

Every morning this woman appeared on the roof. Her fair hair lit up in the sun like corn, and her eyes were green, like young clover in the fields. They jumped here and there like two green grasshoppers before settling down quietly to fasten themselves on her own eyes. If matters had gone no further than that nothing might have happened. But the woman began to smile. At the beginning Ain did not know the smile was meant for her. Throughout her life no one had ever smiled at her, no smile had ever been directed her way. When she used to see a smile on her mother's face and think it was meant for her, she would discover that this was not so. It was always meant for someone else, for a visitor, or for one of the neighbours.

But this smile was meant for her, not for someone else. She would be standing in the door of the tent alone, with nobody at her side, nobody in front or behind. She knew she was alone in the tent. Nevertheless she would turn round to make sure that no one was standing behind her, that the smile was not meant for someone who might happen to be in her proximity.

Her lips did not know how to part in that special way that produces a smile. They were always pressed one against the other, and her mouth was always tightly shut. It was as though she had only one lip, instead of two. Whenever she was seized with that obscure feeling of suffocation, she parted her lips slightly to let out a muffled, almost inaudible, scream but her lips never really parted, never left a space between them. What she used to do was purse them so that they protruded in front. If she ventured to wet them a little with her tongue they sometimes formed a very narrow slit through which her white teeth would flash like a sudden ray of white light lasting for a moment.

This time, however, she returned the smile with a smile which resembled it in many ways. Perhaps it was not really like it. It might not even have been a smile at all. But she succeeded in making her jaw muscles contract and relax so that her mouth opened, exposing two rows of small, white teeth.

*

It did not seem as though the woman was bestowing anything else on her, apart from a smile. Yet the truth is that she was getting something very precious from her, something the woman did not know how to hide. Before all this happened nobody had ever given her anything. So now she had the feeling that she was not taking something, but stealing it. This made her anxious and her movements became agitated since she felt she might be caught stealing what was not hers to have.

In the morning after waking up, when she approached the door of the tent to open it, her hands were not as steady as before. Sometimes they even trembled. She used to stand upright behind the narrow slit as though spying on someone. When the woman appeared on the roof she started to smile in her direction. Ain would look behind her as though making sure that there was nobody standing there, then turn around to face the woman. When they smiled at one another it was as though they were engaged in some sinful traffic. She would close the slit in the tent immediately after, like someone hiding the evidence of a crime.

At the start it might have been possible to put a stop to this dangerous game, but after a while she could no longer do it. Her eyes would be fastened on the opening in the door as soon as she woke up in the morning. If the woman was a little late in appearing she would become anxious and start pacing from one side of the tent to the other, her eyes fixed on the slit-like opening. Once the daily exchange of smiles was over she would fasten up the door and wait for the following morning when she could go straight to the door, open it up and wait for the woman.

If what was happening had been just a game invented by her imagination it might have gone on like that without changing. But it was not simply a product of her imagination. The woman was a real woman made of flesh and blood whom she could see moving and speaking in front of her. So the day came when what had to happen happened, the day when Ain opened the door of the tent to find herself face to face with the woman standing outside. Here it becomes difficult to describe what happened after that. The moment was a complicated one, and Ain's feelings were even more complicated. Should she close the door or open it, know this woman or not know her, want her or refuse her? The door kept opening and closing, although she neither opened it nor closed it but stood immobile, holding the flap with trembling fingers, opening and closing it in her mind. She could have remained like that indefinitely were it not for the clear ringing voice that went through her ears, sharp as a bell.

'I am your neighbour, Noon. Can I come in?'

'Come in.'

Ain did not know how it was that her lips had parted to let out the words 'Come in.' The tone of the woman when she asked her question meant she was seeking permission to enter. This was the first time in her life that anyone had asked her permission. Things had always been forced on her like threatening blows, and all she could do was accept them. If people had asked her permission or asked her what she thought she might have found them more easy to accept, or even have welcomed them of her own free will. But nobody had ever considered she had a will of her own, or feelings that had to be taken into account.

And so Noon walked in through the door, her green eyes shining with that special light as they looked around the tent. She was tall and upright, her body supple as it moved in smooth, powerful waves, her fair hair falling over white shoulders, her full, moist lips parted slightly to expose her small, regular, white teeth.

'What is your name?'

'Ain.'

'Ain El Hayah?'*

'Ain.'

'Names are sometimes made shorter.'

'Shortened?'

'As a way of petting.'

'Petting?'

'Yes. Fatima is changed to Foufou, Nefissa to Nounou, and Ain El Hayah to Ain.

'Ain?'

'But I will call you "Ain El Hayah".'

* *Ain El Hayah* in Arabic means The Well of Life.

'Ain El Hayah?'

'Because you resemble Ain El Hayah.'

'Who, me?'

'Ain El Hayah was my only friend.'

'Only her?'

'She went away.'

'Went away?'

'I loved her more than myself . . .'

'Yourself.'

'. . . and she used to love me in the same way.'

'The same way.'

'The years have passed but her features are still vivid in my mind.'

'Her features?'

'Her features were very much like your features.'

'My features?'

'Your shining, black eyes.'

'Shining?'

'And your tall, full figure.'

'Full?'

'And your clear, dark skin.'

'Dark?'

'And your smooth, black hair.'

'Smooth?'

'Under her eyebrow she had a beauty spot like you.'

'Beauty spot?'

'I mean this little raspberry.'

'Raspberry?'

'When a mother has a longing to eat something it ends up by showing on her baby's skin.'

'Baby?'

'Perhaps your mother longed for something.'

'My mother?'

'Perhaps she longed for an apple.'

'Apple?'

'Your cheek is like an apple.'

'My cheek?'

'An apple hanging from a tree.'

'Hanging?'

'You must have heard of such things before.'

'Before?'

'Someone must have told you about them.'

'Someone?'

'Perhaps your husband . . .'

'My husband?'

'. . . or someone dear to you.'

'Dear to me?'

'Perhaps your lover.'

'My lover . . .?'

It was as though she were learning how to talk. The names were strange to her, the words new. They went through her head like splinters of hot iron that leap out flaming from under the ironsmith's hammer. She kept opening and closing her mouth, repeating the same thing under her breath a hundred times. 'Ain El Hayah, Ain El Hayah . . . Ain El Hayah.' She did not know why these words in particular continued to echo unceasingly in her mind. Perhaps because they sounded easy and familiar, since her name was a part of them; not a small part, in fact, but one half or perhaps more than half. For what could the name 'Ain' all by itself mean? Perhaps her father had forgotten to write down her name in full, or after he had written it down had forgotten to pronounce the second half when he called her and this had gone on.

It was as though she had suddenly found out the last half of her name. She continued to repeat to herself 'Ain El Hayah', 'Ain El Hayah' and now it seemed that she had also found the lost half of her own self. Up until that moment she had not been living with her whole self, but with only half of it. Ain had been only half a human being, but now she was Ain El Hayah, a complete human being.

And so Ain started to become Ain El Hayah, to take her over. It was not a simple change that made her realize that she was now someone else. It was a kind of fusion – not even a fusion but something more, a negation, a disappearance of something, as when it unites with something else, or metamorphoses into something else, like a caterpillar into a butterfly. This process was not a conscious one, one of which she was aware and which she could remember, but rather a change akin to reincarnation, as though 'Ain' had died and had been reborn to live another life in the body of 'Ain El Hayah'.

Or perhaps right from the start she had really been 'Ain El Hayah' and all she had had to do was to rid herself of the other, of the body of 'Ain'.

Everything around her now made her certain that this was true, that it was real. The mirror started to reflect her new image, an image of black, shining eyes, a tall, rounded body, a dark, clear skin, silky hair, and a beauty spot under her left eyebrow. But what made her certain also was Noon's voice calling out her name at every moment; and, all day long, Noon's green eyes encircling her, besieging her, following her insistently to tell her that she was really Ain El Hayah.

For her there was no longer anything else in life that counted, except this truth about herself. Admittedly, there still existed that creature who lived with her, but he remained only a creature whose species and sex were unknown. Every night the thin, narrow chest would wheeze with the usual long, drawn-out cough, and the soft, heavy paw, damp with sweat, would reach out for her. Every morning she still pushed the flaccid, trembling foot into its shoe after he had accorded her the usual kicks and curses.

He continued to be there, as he always had been, like a natural phenomenon, a part of the universe, or a character in a play acting his role day after day. His coughing neither increased nor diminished. His feet and hands were always moist with sweat, always intruding, always flaccid, slow, creeping. Everything about him remained as it was – amorphous, formless like mud or dough. Can a piece of mud or dough feel what is going on around it? Notice change? Can it realize that the sky is now a deep, clear blue without a single cloud in it? Can it discern any difference between a woman Seen or Sheen, between a woman Ain and a woman Ain El Hayah?

But Noon was able to find her friend, to bring her back after she had been lost. Noon was a woman who knew what life was. Not ordinary, everyday life in which men marry women, fathers have sons, and where order reigns thanks to official papers and certificates. Noon knew nothing about that kind of life. She had never married, never had children. No one had given birth to her, and she had never held an official document or certificate – even a birth certificate – in her hands.

Then how was she born? She did not know. No one knew. Perhaps an unknown woman had given birth to her, and died. Or perhaps she had wriggled out of the earth like a worm, or emerged from some living creature by a chance mutation of nature. No one knew anything about her origins, or how she had grown up. Yet here she was, living as though she had opened her eyes one fine morning to find herself in the world.

If she had chanced on another place perhaps she would not have known what to do with her body. Then she might have wandered like a lost creature eating grass until she died. But she had come into existence in a strange place that was not so very strange, since it was known to many people. Nevertheless, it did look different from ordinary places. There was not much space, and it was very crowded. The little houses huddled up against one another until their walls stuck together and formed a single mass. There were no streets but only very narrow tortuous alleys, so narrow that only a single human body could pass at a time. People stood in single file, one behind the other, forming long, thin lines which advanced very slowly through the tortuous alleys, so slowly that at times it looked as though they had not moved a single step in the queue.

This close proximity between people caused no problems in the queues, since they were all men. Or perhaps they were not men: who knows? They had shaven heads, long beards and bushy whiskers, and their chests and legs were covered with thick hair. They stood in the queues waiting for their turn. If the queues advanced very slowly, or even not at all, they would squat or lie on the ground, and sometimes even closed their eyes for a drowse or a nap which might last for some time.

Their sleep was not a normal sleep, for in normal sleep one loses consciousness of what is happening around one; but they knew what was happening all the time, as though they were not asleep at all. They were not in a state of full consciousness but hanging somewhere halfway, half conscious.

Perhaps they were drunk, or in coma or a similar state. There was one thing, however, which never escaped their attention; one thing they seemed to follow steadfastly with eyes wide open. The body. It could be seen on the high roof at the very end of the narrow valley. It was just a body, but it kept waving to them. It was as though this body were the common goal on which all the long lines of people advancing slowly in the alleys converged, as though it were the one aim of this mass movement of human beings who strove and struggled, hour after hour, day after day, perhaps year after year, to arrive at.

It was only a body; nevertheless it was not just any body. It was a woman's body. Probably all the houses huddled together in this place were full of women's bodies. But these were not really women's bodies. These were the bodies of wives, made acquiescent by force of law. A man could marry one, two, three, or four bodies at a time and yet somehow feel more and more deprived, less and less satisfied, just as a sick and inflamed stomach feels a growing thirst with every drink of water. Or perhaps it was not a deprivation they felt but a continuous hunger and lust for everything out of reach or forbidden.

Sick they could be yet not knowing the reason for their sickness. It could be the suffocating lack of air in the narrow, crowded alleys, or the strict law which obliged them to line up one behind the other, or the terrible feeling that the queue was not moving and that they might spend their lives in the same place, waiting.

It was here, in this strange place, that Noon discovered her body. It was not just an ordinary body. It was tall and upright with full, pointed breasts and a waist which narrowed for some distance, to widen further down over the rounded buttocks. She had nothing in life except her body, so she started to educate it. She did not know exactly how to educate it, so she started to move it, and when she moved it, it moved. When she stretched out her arms they went full-length over her head, and when she shook her buttocks they shook. If she bent her waist it yielded, and when she lifted her legs they rose high in the air. So she started to dance; but when she danced it was not the usual kind of dancing, performed as a duty because paid for with money. Her body danced as though, when dancing, it were breathing, living, as though dancing were nature and its nature to live the dance, to move in that way, to bend and twist, to wring itself dry of every drop of sweat, of sweet-smelling sap.

When men started to throw themselves at her, Noon did not see herself as an immoral woman. She did not know the meaning of morality; or perhaps she understood morality in a different way. Morals, in her mind, were something that helped her to live, helped her to love life, and made life open its arms to her. She felt that a woman who attracted men so much that they went after her in droves could only be a moral woman; that a woman who did not do that to men, or attracted only a handful of men, could only be immoral.

In any case, she did not bother too much with finding a name for things. She was not in need of that. She had everything. Life, with its riches, its pleasures and its men, stood outside the door of her house and it was for her to choose whether to open the door or keep it closed. If she threw one man out, then two came along, and if she threw out two, then four rushed up. They multiplied like flies in the heat.

Men were no more than flies that settled for a while, then flew off. She had no one else except her friend Ain El Hayah. She loved her. It was not an ordinary love, in which lovers remain separate beings. It was that wonderful feeling that Ain El Hayah was so close to her that she was almost a part of her; that she would eat when she ate, drink when she drank, sleep when she slept. So close that she would move her arm when she moved her arm, and bend her waist when she bent, and shake her buttocks when she shook them, and lift her legs up in the air when she lifted her legs. Things had gone so far between them that Ain El Hayah might have imagined she was Noon and Noon that she was Ain El Hayah, were it not for the difference in the colour of their eyes and hair. For apart from that they were like twins.

However, they were not twins. Their mother was not the same mother, their father not the same father.

The Well of Life

Perhaps this was why another difference between them showed up later, after Ain El Hayah had moved to live with her in her house. At that time Noon did not know that Ain El Hayah had fled from the tent in which she was living. Ain El Hayah had become Ain El Hayah and the tent could no longer be a home for her. Her home had now become wherever she lived. So when she walked the distance to Noon's house it was with a calm, unhurried gait, with a firm and natural step as though she were just walking home.

When Noon used to look at her, it was as though she were seeing herself; when she saw Ain El Hayah's body it was as though she were looking at her own body and not at the body of someone else. Ain El Hayah's body was younger and more supple, yet it was the same body which Noon saw when she looked at herself.

Ain El Hayah could easily have continued to live this way, were it not for the fact that she was not Noon but a woman made of a different stuff.

The day came when for the first time in her life Ain El Hayah met a man. She did not know what the word 'man' meant. Her father was not a man; he was her father. Her husband? What had her husband been? She did not know. She could not even remember. When she had asked Noon to describe a man for her, Noon had answered her in obscure words, the meaning of which she did not comprehend. 'Eyes with a piercing look which goes through the heart like a revolver shot. After that the body bends like a tree branch, yields gradually under the weight of its fruit. That wonderful exhilaration which makes the senses live, and that magic moment when the body is no longer a body, the head no longer a head, the leg no longer a leg, when all of them become a bundle of electric waves and nerves all interlaced, a network that has throbbed since the beginning of time, and will throb to the infinite end. A mesh of pleasure and energy, of shocks and thrills which seems as though it can never come loose to create a separate man and woman again.'

Ain El Hayah had understood nothing of all this. She stretched out her long supple body on the ground. She could feel the warm earth under her back, see the sky with no stars, just velvet black. She did not know what she should do, close her eyes or open her lids and look out. She hesitated for a moment, then decided that it was best to open one eye and close the other. The dark was pitch black but some light filtered through from an opening, somewhere in the night. It was enough for her to see the broad chest, the hair bristling from his neck and down over his chest like a dark, mysterious forest, then over his belly, tense as a drum. She lay there watching, without movement, wondering what came next.

Suddenly a huge, heavy mass weighed down on her

as though a wall had collapsed over her. She tried to open her mouth, to let out a scream, but something like an iron vice was clamped over her lips. She tried to breathe but her nose was squashed flat on her face, and no air could move in or out through it. Her muscles were seized by violent spasms, as happens when a living body is deprived of air and hovers on the verge of death. After a while the spasms subsided and her body became still. Not a muscle in it moved, not an arm or a leg or an eyelid.

One might have thought she was dead, but she was not. What had come over her was not really death, but something else preceding it, a clinical death in which respiration ceases but the heart continues to contract in an imperceptible beat which the ear cannot detect. It may continue for some time; in fact it may continue for a long time. It is not easy for a living body, for a human being, to die, especially if it is a woman. Besides, she was not an ordinary woman; she was Ain El Hayah with that wonderful body of hers, two rounded, smooth, white breasts moulded out of mud, two huge eyes made out of pools of waste water yet limpid as a mountain lake, the pupils standing out, black and shining like precious stones set on a milky white tissue.

It was not easy for her to bear a suffocation close on death. The heavy mass still lay like a wall upon her. Were it smooth, perhaps its weight might have been more bearable. It was rough, with tortuous furrows on its surface, and sharp ridges. It had small, hard, pointed protrusions like pinheads which grazed her skin. Yet she might have been able to stand all this were it not for the sense of terrible humiliation which she felt was destroying her soul.

She reached a stage where for her all consciousness was lost. Yet it was not so much a loss of consciousness as a suffering which gripped her to the exclusion of all other feelings, and even went beyond the threshold where it could itself be felt. It was like a fire which burns everything, and ends by burning itself out, leaving nothing but ashes.

Nevertheless, she was not a fire which could burn itself out. She was Ain El Hayah. The wall had to go, had to leave her to herself. At a certain moment she suddenly felt it was no longer there, that she was rid of it. How this happened she did not know, but she knew she was rid of it, could no longer feel its pressure on her. It left her nose squashed like a butterfly flattened between the pages of a heavy book, like a piece of meat made as thin and translucent as the finest sheet of paper by repeatedly pounding it with a heavy butcher's knife.

Her delicate lips were bleeding. They showed the marks left by the teeth of the iron vice. Her nose seemed almost to have gone back to its normal place but not quite. It was slightly displaced, or was leaning a little to one side. All over her body were small scratches and bruises which slowly exuded a reddish fluid, and in the midst of all this was that wound, a deep gash from which came a continuous flow of blood.

She rested her hand on the ground, ready to raise herself and get up. She glimpsed a small, green ten-piastre note lying nearby, and her sharp pointed nails reached out to snatch it up. No sooner had she made this move than she found Noon standing in front of her, smiling as usual with her full, moist lips slightly parted.

She managed to get up, but now her movements were heavy. Her waist was no longer as supple as before. The wall had gone and everything she had felt could have disappeared with it completely had it been just a wall. But the wall was not a wall. It was a man with a body made of flesh and blood. He had glands which could inject deep into her body, and other glands which left the odour of his sweat on her skin.

The smell of him lingered in her nose for some time, although she could not remember how it had come. Now everything seemed to be strange. She would turn and throw a rapid glance around her, as though wondering where she was. She felt that what had happened was just her imagination; had in fact not happened at all. Things were getting confused. She could not see them clearly, distinguish one thing from the other, separate between right and wrong. When she looked at her exhausted body in the mirror she felt that Ain El Hayah was gone, that she was no longer the woman she had known. She remembered that her nails were pale, unpainted and cut short. Now her nails were scarlet red, long and pointed at the tips, ready to tear things apart. They were not the fingers of Ain El Hayah, nor were the eyes her eyes, for the lashes were heavy with kohl. When she patted her mop of dyed hair she felt it was not her hair any more, and when she touched her belly she felt it was the belly of another woman, a stranger with whom she had yet to acquaint herself. Yet it was her belly all right. It kept growing all the time until it reached her chest. It was no longer the small rounded belly that stood out gently above her pubic hair; but it was her belly, there was no doubt about that.

She could no longer bend at the waist. Her belly had grown so much that it almost stuck to her chest. Now she had no waist. When she moved her legs, she could feel the shock in her belly, for it had grown in all directions, overlapped to rest itself on her thighs.

Noon's eyes circled round her body like green grasshoppers, searching for her waist. The flashing smile which had shone between her lips no longer flashed out. It had disappeared; why, she did not know. All she knew was that her waist had disappeared, and with it had disappeared Noon's smile. Before long Noon had disappeared too. She had never thought that this would happen. Noon was a part of herself, like her belly or her chest or her waist or her head; so how was it that she had gone?

Her waist had disappeared, how she did not know.

It had been a supple, obedient waist. When she had
wanted it to bend, it bent, and when she had wanted it
to twist, it twisted like a piece of soft locoum, or chewing
gum. She loved her waist perhaps more than anything
else, more than she loved Noon. It was her waist which
was the link between the upper half of her body and the
lower half. Her waist could have meant everything to her
were it not that later on she discovered something else.

What was that something else? She could not tell
exactly. Some time before, she had discovered the other
half of her name, and the half of herself which had been
lost. Now what she discovered was not a half but a
whole, a complete and perfect whole. At first she thought
that this whole could only be 'Allah'. She had heard this
word pronounced before, but she did not know what it
meant. In some vague way she had felt that this word
meant something bigger than herself, or her father, or
her mother, bigger than anything else she had ever
known. So when she first met Noon the thought occurred
to her that Noon must be Allah. Later, she discovered
that her own body was younger and more versatile than
Noon's and she began to feel that Allah dwelt within
her, had made her body his abode. But now, suddenly,
she had found something bigger than herself. That
something, therefore, could be nothing less than Allah
Himself.

But after giving it some thought she decided that it
was not Allah. It was something different, something

wonderful she could feel lying deep inside her body. It pulsated softly with her pulse, had a soft warmth like the warmth of her flesh, and soft, smooth movements that thrilled her to her innermost depths. At night when everything was silent he would begin to knock on the wall of her belly with his tiny, delicate hands. This knocking gave her an extraordinary feeling. It was as warm as the flow of her blood, as soft and smooth as her liver. His whispers mingled with her breathing and she asked herself: Is he saying anything? She would strain her ears to hear him, caress her belly with the palm of her hand, moving it over her liver up to her chest. When she felt the tiny pressure of his hands under her palm she shuddered. Was he a God alive in her entrails? He was not any God; he was her God. She had created him. He was the only thing she possessed; he was hers and hers alone. Never before had she possessed anything. Never had anything been hers. Others had possessed her, owned her. Her father, her mother, her husband. Men. Even Noon had owned her like a thing, like property.

For the first time in her life she now owned something. Not a tent or a pot or a robe, but a God. Her unique God whose tender spirit was capable of dispelling the silence that surrounded her, capable of instilling warmth in her body and her heart. He was her beloved son, the only thing she owned in the world.

It was as though she had never known sadness. Her

old sadnesses were no longer sadness. Her past life, with all its suffering, seemed as though it were the life of another woman, who had lived and died only to hand over to her the reward for all her suffering. This reward was precious, so precious that it was more valuable than what she was carrying inside her, even though it filled her to the brim and overflowed.

Every time she felt herself overflowing with happiness, she would turn round and look behind her as though she felt that someone were hunting her down, as though the other woman, who had died, had awakened suddenly and was running after her, intent on demanding the price of her suffering. She got so frightened sometimes that she would start to walk fast, all the time looking around her, hiding her belly with her arms as though she was trying to conceal something she had stolen, something she had taken even though she had no right to it.

What was it that was hunting her down? She did not know. It was certainly not that woman. In fact it was not a woman at all; it was a man. Sometimes he did not take on the image of a man. Nevertheless, without a doubt he was a man. Sometimes he was tall and thin, with narrow eyes. The eyes had no eyelashes, and they resembled those of her father. Sometimes he was short and thickset, panting behind her. His breathing was almost a wheezing cough. His feet on the ground were heavy and soft like the padded feet of a camel. There were times when he was not one man, but the bodies of many men joined in a single mass, out of which jutted the heads, and the arms, and the legs, like an octopus or a strange animal risen from the ocean depths.

She now wore a large, wide robe which hid her belly. She walked quickly, moving from rock to rock, from tree to tree, so as to hide herself. The small hands kept knocking at her belly. They were not the usual delicate knocks which ceased after a short while, but a continuous, insistent, almost savage knocking which shook her body and seemed almost to split her down the middle. Perhaps she was really being split right down the middle, for how else could she explain the pain she was experiencing for the first time? It was like a saw which kept working up and down from the top of her head to the tips of her toes, passing from her chest to her belly and over to her back. She opened her mouth to scream but instead, to prevent herself, quickly put her hand in her mouth and closed her jaws over it with all her strength so that her teeth bit into its flesh.

In a split second everything was over. The saw passed through her body into space and fell to the ground. Her body, split in halves, lay on the ground bleeding slowly. All this happened in one short moment which seemed to last no more than one or two seconds. Yet it also seemed to last an eternity, to traverse her whole life from the moment she was born – or even before, when she was still an embryo fighting for survival, without teeth, or nails, or hair – right through the stages of her life, from the moment she came into existence as a female child, a girl, till the girl became a woman, and the woman a mother ready to give birth.

Motherhood coursed through her warm, bleeding body with a sensation of heaviness, of cold, like an icy cold current of air going through it. It made her shiver. She wound her arms and legs around her body, seeking warmth, only to find herself embracing a tiny human creature. It had eyes which resembled her eyes, and hands and feet which resembled her hands and feet. It was as though she were looking at him through a lens which made everything look smaller. She enfolded him even closer, with her arms, her breasts, her legs, her lips, with every part of her body. It was as though she were embracing her own body, touching her skin with her lips wherever she could move her face close to it.

He was gasping for breath, and his small mouth was open, so she put her nipple into it. When she felt the smooth, weak clench of the jaws over her nipple she embraced him even more closely with her body as though trying to take him back into her belly once more. Perhaps she was really trying to take him back into her body, for at that moment an icy wind blew in from every direction. His small body started to shiver, and his delicate, pink skin turned into a dark blue. If she could only have kept him inside her belly for ever! Suddenly she leapt to her feet, all the time looking around her. The hunt was still on. Now it had become more savage than ever. There were more people after her. In fact there were so many of them that she could see them standing in a long line, the front of each one of them pressed up against the back of the other. The long, narrow line of people was advancing towards her, and they were all men. Perhaps they were not men in the real sense of the word but in any case their heads were shaven, they had long beards and whiskers, and their chests and legs were covered with thick, black hair like a dense forest.

She wondered whether they were the same men who had crowded the alley leading to her door, the same men who had waited for their turn hour after hour. She was not sure, for this time they were not waiting, they were not eyeing her in anticipation. They were advancing towards her in what looked like a violent, savage attack.

So she started to run. She did not know where to go but she ran. First she took off her shoes, so that nobody could follow the thud of her feet on the ground, sealed her wound with a handful of dust so that no one could follow the trail of blood she left behind, and clapped her hand over the small mouth so that no one would hear the screams of the child. Then she ran. She kept turning round to look behind. At moments she thought she had escaped the pursuit, only to find herself in sight of their eyes, as she ran over open ground with nothing to hide her. Then all of a sudden she found herself poised over the waters of a river flowing by.

Here she stopped. She could see the powerful flow of dark water in front of her, and could hear the sounds of the mad pursuit coming up behind her. Now she was trapped, unable to go on, unable to go back. The wound had drained her of all blood, had bled her white. Her brain was white, its cells were white, her face was as white as a sheet. Her body was exhausted, no energy left, no strength. She felt desperate, lost. She started to shiver with fear, not an ordinary fear, the familiar, habitual fear we have all known. It was a terrible fear, more terrible than any other. It was the fear that a woman or man can only feel when, for the first time in life, for the last time in life, they know that death is close on their heels. A fear that awakened a giant, savage strength that knew nothing else, saw nothing else, was blind to everything except itself.

Right in the middle of this fleeting, fleeing, never-before-lived moment, the child let out a piercing scream. She was seized with panic, tried to shelter him, to quieten him, to hide him in her bosom. But he continued to scream, to kick frantically. She hugged him more and more closely to her bosom, as though trying to enclose him in the folds of her body, to suck him up into her belly where he had been before. If only he could go back, so that no one would see him, or hear him any more! If only he would remain quiet, stop moving or making a noise, she could wrap him in her clothing like a bundle of garments, or pretend that he was nothing else than a few cobs of maize corn she was carrying in the folds of her robe. But the newborn, naked child was shivering from cold, screaming at the top of his voice, like a wailing siren that refused to stop. The giant within her let go, broke out. She clamped a powerful hand over the small, soft mouth, intent on stifling his screaming for ever, but her other hand was quicker, came up and pulled it off from where it had fastened itself. The mouth, free of her hand, opened wide and started to let out one scream after another, each rising up more and more piercing than before. The pursuit was now close on her heels. She was now fully in sight, clearly visible. She was seized with a mad, frantic panic, with an urge for survival more powerful than anything else. With a sudden leap she threw herself forward, leaving the child behind.

Running as fast as she could, she just had the time to twist her neck round and throw a last glance behind her. His small, naked body lay between the rocks, his mouth a small gap gasping for breath. The small eyes looking out, full of tears, reflected the colour of her eyes; his hands and feet, shaped in the shape of her hands and feet, were held out, imploring her help.

After that she lost track of everything. Her body continued to run, impelled by a strange inertia. Perhaps she dropped down on the earth at some spot, exhausted by loss of blood and the distance she had run; or their flaming torches were able to catch up with her and burn her alive; or their hands got hold of her and tore her body to shreds. Perhaps she never found out what happened to her simply because she was occupied with something else, seeing something else, an image that never disappeared from before her eyes, a small, naked body lying between the rocks, its mouth open and gasping for breath, its small eyes filled with tears coloured with the colour of her eyes, its hands and feet shaped like hers stretching out into space, imploring someone to come to their help.

She closed her eyes, opened them again. Once more she could see the body lying, as it always had, between the rocks, its eyes still brimming with tears which neither dried nor dropped out onto the ground, its small hands and feet stretched out, always moving, never quiet, always calling out, imploring someone to come to their help.

Once more she closed her eyes, opened them again, closed them again, opened them again, kept on closing and opening them a hundred times, a thousand times, so that it was as though they were now only blinking, opening and closing so quickly that they did not really open, nor really close, but merely trembled at a rapid, almost regular, rate, their movement unceasing, never at rest. But each time the lids parted for the smallest fraction of a second, the rocks would appear between her eyelids, and lying between them the small, smooth body, with its mouth open, gasping for breath, two small eyes full of tears, two hands and two feet stretched out. It was as though the image was stuck to her retina, had been etched deep down in the depths of her eyes.

Night and day followed one another as usual. But she was not conscious of the alternation which went on. Her lids were always open, or perhaps they were always shut. To her there was no difference between dark and light, no change. She did not feel that anything was happening. All she felt was that she walked, leaning on the walls as she progressed. Sometimes she would fall to her knees, or bend over the ground, or bury her nails in the earth.

She seemed to be looking for something. Yet this looking for something, this search, was different from a usual search in which one knows what one is looking for, knows what one may succeed or fail to find, knows what one has lost. It was a strange kind of search, for she did not know whether she would find what she was looking for, or not. Perhaps deep inside her she knew that she would never find what she was looking for, and yet she went on. Sometimes she would be seen gazing around her with a lost, vacant look in her eyes, as though she had forgotten why she had come.

At times it was as though she were looking for her mother. Her mother's face would appear, hanging some-where in space above her. She could see her big eyes deep in their sockets looking out at her when she was still a child, standing with the tears dropping down over her pinched cheeks. She could glimpse her eyes as she bent over to give her a quick kiss, that kiss which was not a kiss but a fleeting contact between her cheek and her mother's lips. At other times it would be the face of Noon, her green, grasshopper eyes, her full, moist lips parted in a smile which always flashed out in her direction. There were even times when she glimpsed the trembling, flaccid foot which her husband held out for her to push into the shoe, time after time, until finally she succeeded in squeezing it through.

At moments like this the muscles of her face would contract and her lips would part to let through a small smile, or a sigh of regret for the rare moments of happiness she had felt. But immediately afterwards, her eyes would chance on a child suckling at its mother's breast, or holding on to the tail of its mother's dress, or curling its fingers around its father's thumb, or playing, or weeping or eating. Since children are everywhere, she was always seeing one child or another. Every time, her lids would start to tremble in that strange, rapid way and, every time, that image would come before her eyes, the image of a small, smooth body lying between the rocks, its mouth open, gasping for breath, its hands and feet held out to the air as though imploring her to come to its help.

Her mouth would open wide to let out a shriek, and suddenly her body would rush in between the tents as though impelled by an inner force stronger than herself. She would often drop down to her knees on the rocks, start to dig in the earth, then let it run through her fingers.

She never found anything. She would continue to kneel on the earth. Little by little her body would sink to a sitting position. The cool feel of the earth going through her thighs gave her a sensation of infinite rest. Her dry lips would part. She would breathe in huge gulps of air like gasps, or laughter. In fact it might have been laughter, the laughter of a child which has run on its small, bare feet to the edge of a stream, and is wetting its arms and legs, its hair and its neck with cool water.

If she had merely been the heroine of this story she might have continued to live like this for ever, or she might have died, and been buried in the earth to be eaten by worms.

But she was not. She was a real woman; her reality, her truth was not of the kind which, if you approach it, evaporates only to prove that it was false. Her reality was real, her truth was true. Perhaps at a distance it did not seem to be true, but the nearer you drew to it, the more true it became, the more it could be seen through the eyes, felt by the fingers, smelt by the nose. It was a body with an existence of its own, with its own continuity. This body was not an ordinary body. It was the body of Ain El Hayah, of a woman with her own identity, with a will capable of triumphing over everything. Life had not willed her to live, yet she was born, came to life. Death had ordained that she die, or live a living death, but she defeated death and lived, despite all that others willed. She was refused, ostracized, exiled by everyone. No one can pretend he wanted her. She alone wanted herself. If she had not wanted herself, she would never have been born, never have lived, never have continued to live. Where did this will of hers come from? She did not know. Her body had a marvellous capacity for life. When her little finger used to stretch out to the fire and touch it accidentally, her muscles would contract, and her arm pull back in time to save her hand from being burnt. When her stomach was seized with hunger pains, its wall would contract and secrete a nourishing fluid. If she glimpsed a sharp blade gleam in the dark, or saw a wolf or a leopard, her body would shrink, roll up into a small ball, and hide itself in a hole or behind a rock. Her cells were even capable of transforming the small worms, which she used to swallow with mud from the pools of water, into body tissue.

She wanted to live, so she lived. If she had wanted to die, she might have died before she was born, or later, or at any time. But she wanted to live. Perhaps her will to live was stronger than anything else, so it made her live despite everything. The morning sun used to bathe her body as she lay stretched out near the stream. It helped her to grow strong, made her body harden, her feet able to stand the sharp, jutting rocks. When she walked over long distances, a trail of blood, a river of blood, followed behind her. She filled her open wound with dust to stop the blood from flowing, and went on. Whenever she glimpsed something move in the water, on the sands, or over the rocks – be it a fish, a snake, or a small mouse – it would look to her like a small body with its hands and feet stretched out in the air. She would rush towards it, only to discover that there was nothing there. So she would stand there for a while, panting, her eyes moving around, with that look of being lost.

Perhaps her feet often bled from so much walking, her eyes tired from so much staring, her fingers wasted from so much digging. Perhaps she went hungry, or naked, or the rain fell on her, and made her hands and feet freeze with cold. Perhaps they threw refuse and dirt at her. Perhaps anything. She never stopped. She had decided to live, to conquer death. Her refusal was no ordinary refusal in which one refuses but is not sure whether this refusal is final. It was a refusal in which she had no choice. She had been faced with a refusal of herself from others right from the start, and there was no other way for her to go, but to refuse this refusal.

If it were just a matter of fiction, just a product of the imagination, this story might have ended at this point; but the story of this woman was not merely a product of the imagination. She was a woman made of flesh and blood and she had lost a son born of flesh and blood. There was no way out for her. There was no choice for her except to forget him, or to find him. But to forget something, one must have something which reminds one of it. She had nothing which could remind her, and, since she could remember nothing, she could forget nothing. Her memory had been destroyed, scraped away to become smooth and slippery like a bald head, to which nothing can stick, on which nothing can grow.

She might have lost herself through forgetting, were it not that she ended up by finding him there amidst the rocks. Perhaps whoever she found was not him. The mouth was angry, and the eyes were not full of tears but flashed out sparks. The hands and feet were not stretched out for help, but were folded closely round a gun. Yet he resembled him so closely that she was able to recognize him at once. The passage of time, the days and years had exhausted her, humiliated her, so she was incapable of letting out a cry of happiness and joy. All she could do was to let her broken, wounded, bleeding body fall to his feet.

The Thread

This woman haunted me, invaded me, drained me to the point of exhaustion over a number of years. She would come to my clinic in Giza with some complaint or other. The first time it was a pain in the chest. When I examined her I could find nothing wrong. She disappeared for a while then came back one day with a request that I examine her father who lay sick in bed at home. I went with her to his house and found him in such a hopeless state that I could do nothing except alleviate his pain with some injections.

After that she disappeared, only to return again after some time complaining that the pain in her chest kept recurring and that now in addition there was a big swelling in her belly. When I examined her I found her pregnant. I asked her how it had happened. She had no explanation. She begged me to do an abortion, but the pregnancy was now in its ninth month, and I could not intervene.

For a long time I ceased to see her, until one day,

here she was back again, with the same complaint of pain in the chest. Her visits became more and more frequent, but now each time she would complain of pain in a different place. I examined her thoroughly but could find no reason for these shifting pains. When I said this to her she became very angry and raised her fist to strike me. I stepped aside quickly to avoid the blow, and instead of hitting me it landed on a portrait of mine hanging on the wall. The glass was broken but she escaped without a scratch on her hand.

After this incident she kept away. I had no idea what had become of her until, to my great surprise, I found a letter from her in my mail. It read as follows.

My Dear Doctor,

The first time I came to your clinic I had not yet been born. You see in fact I was not really born on the day my mother is said to have given birth to me. I was still no more than a lump of flesh which moved here and there without a will, and without desires of its own. I was being led by another will, by desires other than my own.

Time passed but I did not feel it come or go. Today was no different from yesterday, no different from tomorrow. Past and future were merged into the present, into a single moment lasting for ever. For me time was inexistent.

I know I was born during a particular hour of a cold winter night. However, it did not take me a full hour to be born. To be precise it took no more than seven minutes. Of this I am sure, for I happened to glance at my watch when it all started and I remember the hands were pointing at seven minutes to eleven. I was sitting up in bed writing under the glow of my lamp. I am in the habit of writing for some time before going to sleep. I heard a strange sound. My hand stopped. Was it really a sound I heard or was it something else? If not, how could I have heard it? There was no mistake. Yet it seemed different from any other sound I had heard. It vibrated in my ears, in my whole body. An almost imperceptible movement went through my flesh, through my arms, through the wall of my belly, like invisible waves, or tiny ants creeping over my skin.

With one rapid leap I was in my father's room. Everything was as it had always been. He was lying with his eyes half open, half closed, the white sheet covering the lower part of his body, his arms stretched out weakly by his side, like empty sleeves in an empty coat. His body was completely still. No part of it stirred. Only his eyelids and lips opening and closing in a monotonous, regular movement, the continuous rise and fall of his chest, the slow throb of an artery in his thin, scraggy neck.

Once more I heard the same sound I had heard before. I put my finger over where the artery throbbed, and stood near the bed, unmoving, like a block of stone. My finger pressed down on the artery, frozen stiff. I could see my father's face on one side, his wide forehead protruding above his shrunken face, the beads of sweat which stood out on it, the cheek bones, angular, sharp under the skin, the nose thin and long, overhanging his upper lip where the hairs of his whiskers had fallen out, leaving a dark shadow that moved with his sallow lips in that monotonous regular movement which refused to stop.

To this very moment I can still see his lips open and close, still hear the same moan repeat itself, the blowing sound of his breath going in and out of his nose, the ticking of the clock in the night. They are fused into a single sound, into a weak, weird, desperate, ebbing cry. I do not know when it started. I cannot remember, no matter how much I try, as though this sound had no beginning, no hour or moment at which it started in the silence of the night, as though it started gradually, imperceptibly, so that it never really started but had always been there for as long as I could remember, as though I had never seen my father except in this posture, lying in his bed, never heard any sound from him except the sound of moaning. It was as though all fathers were born like that. An irrevocable situation where all things were linked for all time, just as darkness has to fall with the night, and light has to break with the day, and air has to flow in and out of one's chest.

But I knew that this was not really so. For there was a time in my life when I used to see my father standing upright. Slim and tall, he trod the ground firmly. I can hear the tap-tap of his heels, slow, steady, rhythmic as he advanced on the tarmac road. I can hear his voice when he spoke. His voice was gruff, a man's voice, and yet it was a tender gruffness which I felt in my ears especially when he called out my name. My name, Dawlat, resonated strangely. The D seemed to vibrate in the air with a special vibration. I used to go to school. School was far away and I had to take a train every day, a long train with a sharp whistle and clouds of smoke. I loved this period of my life, why I do not know. Maybe I loved the swaying of the train like a see-saw, the big windows, and the telegraph poles rushing by quickly. Or perhaps it was my father's big, strong hand, and his long fingers clasped over mine as my foot climbed the high step into the train. Or perhaps I loved him even more as I walked by his side along the street leading to the school, while he carried my bag, heavy with books. I was small, close to the ground and could see his big feet treading over it, could see one foot follow the other, slow and sure, as though it knew the exact distance his step had left behind, the exact distance it had to take in front, the exact spot on which it should come down.

Everything around me seemed magical, or maybe that is how I felt about it later on, for not all my childhood was as magical as this. There was a strange feeling which troubled my life. I did not have this feeling every day, but it lay dormant inside me, and would grow for the slightest reason. The sound of my father's foot slipping over a stair, a sudden screech of brakes when he was crossing the road, or the sudden silence when he stopped snoring. Although I knew that he had probably moved his head, or turned over on the other side, yet my body would shake with a deep fear. I feared for my father, feared that he would die. I had never seen a dead person, nor had anyone ever spoken the word 'death' in front of me, yet I knew it well. It was as though it had been born with me, like a leg or an arm, like one of the organs of my body. It was a part of me. I could feel it, I could touch it. And the feeling of it made me shiver in the same way I shivered when my hand accidentally touched my belly, or my breast.

I do not know why I was afraid that my father might die. I did not know how to get to school alone; he was the one who knew. He was the one who bought me food and clothing, who sat at my bedside and told me stories until I fell asleep. I used to forget all my dreams when I woke up in the morning, except one dream which kept coming back. It was a dream in which the train started to pull out of the station before I had time to put my foot up on the step. My father quickly lifted me into the train, then jumped up behind me, but his foot missed the step and hit the empty air, and I saw him fall under the wheels. I would wake up suddenly, bathed in sweat, but once I heard his snores coming from the next room I would murmur a thanksgiving to Allah, turn over and fall asleep again.

In school, when I heard girls say that it was their mothers who had given birth to them, I used to say that it was my father who had given birth to me. I could hear them laugh but I did not care, and even felt a secret pride. All other girls had been born of women but I had been born of a man. Somehow I knew that men did not bear children, but I believed that my father was not like other men and could do anything.

I remember the moment when for the first time I discovered the colour of my father's eyes. He was sitting on the sofa holding my primary school certificate in his hands. Suddenly he lifted his head and looked into my eyes. The colour of his eyes was black but it was not a pure black. Deep down inside was a blue that looked out through the black like the clear water of a lake. I noticed a drop, transparent as distilled water, in the corner of his eye. It trembled, ready to fall from the edge of his lid, then disappeared suddenly, seemed to flow over his eyes, making them shine with a wonderful light.

In those days I did not know what success could mean, what joy it brought. But after that day success was linked, for me, with the light in his eyes, with that blue transparency like a mountain lake, with a crystal drop which washes the eye, there one moment, invisible the next.

For me there was no success in success, no joy in joy, without that light. I used to search for ways to achieve the most trivial success so that I could run panting to him with the proof of it. It was often only a note of merit in basketball, or first aid, or tidiness or behaviour, but I would thrust it into his hands, stand in front of him and look into his eyes, waiting. When I passed my secondary school examination he was away in his village, in Upper Egypt. He was due to return after three days but I could not bear to wait. I travelled all the way to the village and thrust the certificate into his hands. When I glimpsed the clear blue colour, saw the crystal drop evaporate to reveal that wonderful gleam in his eyes, I was lifted up by the same wave of happiness that used to flow through me when I was still a small child. Even when I grew up and passed my graduation exam at the university I did not feel any joy until the moment I sat next to him on the bed. He was still at the beginning of his illness. I brought the certificate close up to his eyes and looked into them. There was a fine mist lying over them which almost hid the blue colour, but he realized what I was looking for, and the mist lifted for a brief moment, so that the clear blue colour could shine out from behind, and the crystal drop appear at the corner of his eye; but it did not evaporate quickly this time. Instead I could see it hesitate for a moment before it fell over the edge of his lid on to the back of my hand, burning hot, like the head of a flaming match.

I knew nothing about sickness. I had never heard the word before, or seen a sick person. Or perhaps I did hear the word mentioned sometimes, and perhaps I did see some sick people, but this happened at a distance from me, in other people's lives, at the other edge of our existence where neither my father nor I were to be found. When I heard the word 'sickness' from my father I did not understand anything. He continued to walk, to drink, to eat. I thought it was something like a headache that comes and goes, like a cold which raises the temperature, causes some discomfort in the chest for a few days but then disappears. When his walk became slower I did not notice it was slower, and when he bought a stick and started to lean on it I did not find this strange, and when he lay in bed and got up only occasionally, the sight of him lying in bed was not unusual, and when he could no longer rise from his bed, and a nurse started to feed him, I still did not feel that very much was wrong. Everything seemed to be happening in a mysterious way, and every day something small would happen, so that the change was almost imperceptible, like water dropping so slowly from a tap that you neither see nor hear it, but one day it fills up the basin and overflows. Or like the wrinkles of time, so few, so fine, that you only notice when they have become deep furrows cutting into the face.

*

My finger continued to press down over his throbbing artery. The strange sound I had heard was still vibrating in my eardrums, spreading all over my body in little shivering waves. I knew it was my father's voice but this time it was not like his voice when it used to call out to me, not like any voice I had heard before. It had something weird, unnatural about it, unlike any voice my ears had been accustomed to hear. It penetrated through the dense layers of habit which had accumulated layer after layer over my ears, thousands of layers, millions of layers one on top of the other so that in the end my ears could no longer hear, as though they were deaf.

For the first time in my life I discovered that my father was sick, that he would lie in bed without moving until the last day of his life, that he was in pain with a pain which was difficult for a human being to bear, a pain so violent that the tissues in his body were disinte-grating layer after layer, that the flesh over his bones was gradually being destroyed, leaving only his skin like a coating of rust, which coarsened, and cracked, and throttled the nerve-endings running through it.

This discovery forced itself upon me so suddenly that it gave me no time to pull myself together. My finger was still pressing down on his artery, which continued to pulsate, but my head was turned away from his face. From the corner of my eye I could glimpse his profile, its outer edge suspended in my line of vision like a fine hair. My finger was icy cold and his artery felt hot. My eyes followed its slow movement, but my finger no longer felt the pulse. I tried to find it, feel it as I had felt it day after day, increased the pressure of my finger. It rolled away from under the tip, so I pressed down on it even more.

I do not know exactly what happened then. I felt the blood drain away from my head, my chest, my thighs, my legs, and collect in my finger. With it, it seemed to drain away all the strength I had and concentrate it in my finger pressing down on the artery. I could no longer feel the pulse but continued to press. My head was clear, cool, drained of its hot blood.

I was fully conscious, able to feel and to see. I watched my long, brown finger pressing down on the artery, watched the artery as it went white. My father's face was also now quite white, but not the usual white of things which are white. It was a strange white which did not emanate from the thing itself, was not a colour in itself but rather a quality of the eye, like a white spot on the black pupil or a white membrane lining the retina.

I glanced at my watch. It was exactly eleven o'clock. Seven minutes had passed since I had heard that weird sound, but it seemed to me like seven hours, or seven days, or even seven years. I looked round the room with amazement. The sound was no longer in my ears, and with it had disappeared the continuous vibration in my eardrums. It was as though there had been some kind of a thick coating in my ear, or a plug which had fallen out suddenly, so that for the first time in my life I could hear sounds, hear the sound of the green bird as he sang. Every day I used to see him on the branches of the tree opposite the window. I used to wonder how he could remain perched on the branch all those long hours without singing, or chirping. I had not heard the voices of birds before, but I knew they had a voice, and that they sang on the branches of trees.

I thought the bird was mute and did not realize that it was I who did not hear.

I rushed out into the street and started to run like a small child who has found out for the first time that she has ears which hear, and eyes which see, and legs which carry her body and can take her anywhere.

I knew no place other than your clinic. I had been to you once before – do you remember? – the day when I took you with me to examine my father. I could see your face on one side as you put your stethoscope on his chest, on his back, and I glimpsed the long artery standing out in your neck. When I looked into your eyes after you had finished examining him, I did not need your elaborate scribbling on the prescription. I knew he would waste away little by little in pain, that he would abandon his body inch by inch to a slow death. One, perhaps two, perhaps three years at the most before his big body would give way completely, and his strong bones crumble into ashes.

I understood everything, for your eyes were tracing before me the course my life would take, and your finger as it lay on my finger pointed to the road of my salvation. Perhaps, like the others, you will deny all this. But I had more courage than you, because he was my father. He was my father, not yours. I was a part of him. I was a part of his body which wasted away in suffering, abandoned itself step by step to death. When I blotted his artery out with my finger I knew I was saving myself, carving out a way for my body to live. I knew I was not alone. I knew you stood by me, could see your finger on mine, pressing hard to open up a passage for my birth, pulling hard to get my body out, inch by inch, and bit by bit.

When I got to your clinic it was closed and the lights were out. I ran along the streets like someone who has no place to go, but I was looking for your house. I wanted to tell you that I had accomplished the task. That I had been your instrument, acting with precision. That I was only a fine instrument yet I had succeeded in doing what had to be done. I was seeking the joy of my success in your eyes. But I did not know the way to your house, so I found myself rushing home into my father's room. I thought he would hold my birth certificate in his big, long fingers, that I would see the blue colour light up in his eyes, and the crystal drop which disappeared and made them shine. But his room was empty, and his bed was empty, and on the small clothes-hanger behind the door I found his coat. It was empty too. So I crept inside it, buried my head in his chest, lifted his arms, and wound them round my body so that they could hold me tight. But they collapsed loosely on either side like the wide sleeves of an empty coat.

I did not know that people are born in pain. I thought people were born without feeling anything. But later I learnt that pain is necessary, and that a person who is not born in pain is not born, that he remains a lump of flesh like an embryo in its mother's belly, moving under a will other than its own, like the millions of particles floating in the air, in the sea and on the land, like gnats and fish and crocodiles, and the millions of people who have not known what pain is.

For the first time in my life I was being moved by a will of my own. It was still a new will, born recently and still weak, yet capable of moving my tall, slim body. When I reached the offices of the newspaper that day I did not smile at anybody. My old smile had always been involuntary, a parting of the lips which happened whenever I met someone, or even something. It might even be a cat miaowing or a dog biting on a piece of bone, or a small mouse, or a lizard running over the ground, yet I would smile. The smile had no particular meaning but it was always there, stuck on my face, like my nose or my mouth.

I sat at my desk to write but could not write one word. I used to edit a special column every day. I would put one word down after the other, make one phrase follow the other, and arrange them in lines, one line below the other, so that when I had finished the white area of paper had become black. I did not know what to say to people, for there was nothing that I really wanted to say. People read my column every day; or perhaps they did not. I never tried to find out. I was not writing so that people would read what I wrote. My conditions of employment did not stipulate that it must be so. The only condition was that I filled the space given to me with words.

That day I did not write a single word. My head was burning hot. The paper in front of me remained a sheet of white, and the pen in my hand refused to move. I was sitting at a desk in a big room. The floor was covered in tiles arranged in squares. I lifted my head and looked at the floor. This was the first time I had noticed the big, white squares. They were well defined, protruding slightly. In one of the squares, in the corner opposite mine, was a man's shoe. The shoe was small with bands of black and white. For a moment I thought that someone had taken it off and left it under his desk, but after a moment I realized that the shoe was shaking, and that above it were a pair of trousers, one leg of which was suspended over the other and was also making a similar shaking movement.

I never thought of people as divided into two separate sexes, male and female. To me the whole world, that is men and women, formed one sex, while my father and myself constituted the other sex. I thought that my father belonged to my sex, that he was not a man, and that I was not a woman. However, I was not completely ignorant of such matters. It was an ignorance sometimes traversed by flashes of understanding which flared up for a moment, and then went out. These flashes, however, did not light up of their own accord; there was always a reason for them. Once I woke up in the middle of the night after a bad dream. I was shaking with fright and, as I was in the habit of doing when still a child, I ran straight to my father's room. He was fast asleep in his bed. The sheet had fallen off him and he lay there completely naked. It was not the first time I had seen him naked. I used to see him sometimes while he was changing his clothes, but when he felt my eyes on him he would turn quickly and put on his trousers. This time my eyes fastened on his body as though it were the first time I had realized he was a man.

Now his masculinity looked odd to me. It made me feel as though he was a man I had never set eyes on before. I looked at my own body and I was seized by what, to me, was an even stranger feeling, that of being a woman, and of being different from men.

It was as though what I saw was reaching me through a dense mist peopled with many ghosts. I was on the verge of throwing myself into his arms as he slept, so that he would wake up to comfort me and caress me, as he always did, but this time he was the cause of my fright. I ran back to my room and buried myself under the blankets. In the morning all that had happened seemed only a frightening dream, and, as with all my other dreams, I forgot it.

However, this forgetting was not complete. At certain moments my father's naked body would suddenly appear in front of my eyes, and sometimes it would be my naked body that I would see. I used to hate the sight of a naked body. It frightened me, and my fright was so great that I would gasp for breath and feel the air go in and out of my chest like a sharp needle.

I used to put my finger where I felt the needle, while you went over my body with your stethoscope. When it settled on my chest, when you pressed your hands over my ribs, I shrieked with pain, but you did not hear me shriek. You looked at me with stony eyes, and I wondered what kind of human being you could be. You are a doctor, that's true, but above all are you not a woman like I am? Like me, do you not hate stripes in a man's shoe, do you not hate a small size in a man's shoe?

I do not think you are like me, I do not think that all a doctor like you would see in a man is the colour of his shoe, or the size of his foot. No doubt you would see other things which are much more important. But then what is it that is more important for you in a man?

It seemed to me that I must have asked you this question because you answered me. You did not say anything, but I understood the look in your eyes. When you refuse to speak you always depend on your eyes. After I left your clinic I started to stare at the men. I never imagined that there were so many men in the world. I had to choose from among them, but I did not know how to choose. Their features seemed all the same, their voices seemed almost the same, the look in their eyes was the same, their trousers were all trousers with two legs.

At the newspaper there was no one, only the man with the small-sized feet and striped shoes. After a while the upper leg started to shake, and the striped shoe, suspended in the air, followed suit. He was always writing but that day he lifted his head which was always bent over his papers and called out to me.

My name echoed in my ear with a strange vibration. Dawlat. It was as though the letters were no longer the same, had been replaced by other letters. The D in particular sounded like another letter, more important, more resonant than before, with a materiality of its own. I could not only hear it in my ear; I could feel it in my skin, creeping over it, making it roughen and become like goose flesh, so that the hair follicles stood up on end. Not only my skin but every part in my body seemed to turn over slowly at the sound of my name. Even the centre point where the fibres, and the chords, and the nerves of my body converge. I could feel it pulsate, revolve like a small marble lodged in my stomach, deep in my flesh, in the bare triangle below my chest which separates between my ribs.

This turning movement in my depths was painful. It was not a sharp, needle-like pain, but a diffuse, rounded pain which was not a real pain but rather a slight movement, a pressure which became almost a stranglehold, but receded once more to become a tiny body buried deep in my belly, like a worm gnawing its way into my stomach wall.

He seemed to sense what was going on inside me. His hand was steady, experienced, knew its way. It went straight for the gnawing pain inside me. I felt it settle under my chest, over the bare triangle of flesh between my ribs. It was firm and strong, cold like a piece of ice on a burning forehead.

I put my hand on my forehead. My head felt cool, calm. The sky overhead was now a deep blue colour, like the deep blue sea. The tree leaves were green with a green which was fresh, and clean. Everything seemed to have put on new colours. When I walked in the streets my feet moved faster. I wanted to see you. I wanted you to see me. I wanted you to look into my eyes, and find out that I had done what you wanted me to do. Although only your instrument, I had succeeded in fulfilling my assignment. I wanted to read in your eyes the joy of my success. You were not in your clinic, and I did not know the way to your house. Why have you always hidden it from me? I rushed back home to my father's room. I thought I could tell him what had happened to me, what I had succeeded in doing, see my happiness glow in his eyes. But his room was empty, and his bed was empty, and his coat hanging on the hook behind the door was empty. So I stood like a statue and stared at its lonely emptiness.

I still went daily to my office at the newspaper. Every day I found the small, striped shoe under the desk, and a leg crossed over another, shaking in a trouser leg in front of me. Every day he lifted a face which was bent over his papers and my name would echo in the air: 'Dawlat.' But now the letters no longer sounded import-ant, no longer had that special resonance. In particular the D. It had become no more than that ordinary *dal* one hears in an ordinary word like *dawla* or *doush* or *dilw*.* It no longer made my skin become like goose flesh, no longer made the centre point in my body turn over.

He started to call me other names with different letters. Each time he would look for something different, something rougher and more resonant which I could feel creeping over my skin, which would make me quiver, make the hairs in my skin stand out with goose flesh.

* *Dal* is the Arabic letter D; *dawla* – state; *doush* – shower; *dilw* – pail.

One day, in search of a new roughness, a new resonance, he slapped me on the face. No one had ever slapped me on the face. When still in school I had been rapped on the knuckles, or the knees, but never slapped on the face. This slap seemed very odd to me. His cold hand hit the bones of my face, but I felt no pain. I felt a dampness, a wetness on my cheek. It was like spit, but I did not take out my handkerchief to wipe it off. The damp, wet feeling filled me with pride. I lifted my eyes and looked him in the face. It was flat and featureless like the palm of a hand. I closed my lips tightly and swallowed; my saliva had a bitter taste. The bitterness flowed down in my chest and settled in my stomach. I could almost feel it with the palm of my hand where it lay under the wall of my belly. At the beginning it was a small, circumscribed bitterness, like a grain of corn, or a small marble which gave way under the pressure of my fingers, and disappeared somewhere inside, but it soon surfaced again, and I could feel it move under my hand. It kept twisting round on itself like a worm, and sometimes I could feel it bite. I tried to squash it under my hand but it wriggled away, made itself small, then slipped down to some deep place right at the bottom. It never kept still, but kept digging and scratching and pinching, and pushing out its snout inside my stomach, spewing liquid as hot and bitter as gall into my chest. The liquid rose in my throat and mingled with my saliva. I tried to spit it out, but it stuck like glue, and even when I vomited to empty my stomach it remained inside like salt water from the sea.

That day I refused to be convinced by you. I could not believe that children came out from a sea of bitterness. I left the clinic without paying you your fee of one pound, and went to my office in the newspaper. I had stopped writing, stopped filling in my column, but I had nowhere else to go. When I got there everything was gone. The small, striped shoe under the desk was no more to be found. The desks had gone also, and the squares on the ground looked strange without desks. The faces too looked strange. Everything was changed, as though I had come to another place, a place to which I had never been before.

My body was heavy and swollen but I continued to walk in the direction of my home. At the door I put my hand in my pocket for the key, but the key was not there. I knocked on the door three times so that my father would recognize my knock. I saw the door open, but the face that looked out was not that of my father. It was a face that did not know me; a face I did not know.

I returned to your clinic. It was closed and the lights were out. I was unable to walk any further, so I sat down on the pavement in front of the clinic. After a while I could not sit any more. My swollen belly was in the way so I lay down on my back. I started to feel pain in my spine and tried to turn over on my side, but something like a strange body started to creep down in my belly, dropping like a knife that cut its way through my flesh. I was about to scream, but I was afraid that people would hear my screams, wake up, open their windows, and lean out, see me there where I lay. My thighs were uncovered, and under them had collected the bitter water, forming a small pool. I did not imagine that my body was capable of storing so much unclean water. I looked round. All the houses were closed and dark. The street was silent and the cold, night wind whipped my hot body. My head was so hot that my brain inside seemed to dissolve, liquify. I was unconscious of what went on around me, except when I could feel the cold wind buffeting my body, like slops of water poured on hot steel.

I regained consciousness for a short moment when I felt a strong blow hit my belly like a punch. It lifted me up off the ground and dropped me violently down again. I heard the sound of the bones in my skull hit the tarmac road. I put my hands up to my head and found it in its place. I went over my arms and legs, and the ground underneath me. Suddenly my fingers hit against a small, smooth head that lay on the pavement.

My fingers trembled at the feel of this head. They had never felt a head as small as this, soft and smooth with a smoothness which seemed to cling to them, creep up over my arms and shoulders, then over my breasts and my neck to flow into my tongue like warm saliva. This smoothness, this warm saliva, had a special flavour to it like nectar or mellow wine. I sipped it up slowly, savouring it without swallowing, keeping it in my mouth, until it was absorbed drop by drop.

As I absorbed this flavour all the bitterness which had accumulated inside me and filled my mouth with its taste over the years dissolved, leaving no trace behind. My body became light as a feather. I did not know that hatred can lie deep inside the body like a heavy stone.

I was still stretched out on the pavement. Everything around me was silent, motionless. The sky hung over my head and the stars trembled in its dark expanse. In the distance I could see a tall tree, its dense shadow merging in the darkness of the night. Whenever the cool night breeze stirred, it swayed the branches of the tree, and the starry night seemed to tremble more than it had before.

My eyesight had become so sharp that it could penetrate through the dense darkness of the night. Above the black sky there seemed to be a blue expanse, deep blue like the colour of the sea. I was in Alexandria, swimming in the sea. My arm held on to my father's neck as it used to do when I was still a child. The waves carried me up and down with him. Whenever a very big wave came along it lifted me up until my head touched the heavens, then dropped me down into the depths of the earth. I laughed loudly in a shrill, excited, childlike voice.

I could almost hear the sound of my childish

laughter. After a little while I felt sure I was actually hearing it, the gasping sound I used to make when the laughter blocked my nose and my father could not tell whether I was laughing or crying. The sound of it kept echoing in my ears. I waited some time for it to stop, but in vain. I turned round to the place from which it came, and glimpsed a small girl whose features resembled mine when I was still a child. At first I thought it was just a picture, but she was crawling towards me on her belly. I stretched my finger out towards her, thinking it would only meet with air, but five tiny fingers curled round it like a thread of silk. A current of electricity shot up to my shoulder, then moved over to my chest, down to my belly and thighs. My muscles were seized with contractions, my legs and arms bent towards my chest, so that my body formed a cavity into which she crept as though she were familiar with it and it had been made to fit her exact size and contours.

My warmth enveloped her small body. Her tiny fingers ceased to tremble. Blood flowed into her thin, pinched, blue-coloured lips. She parted them slightly, leaving a slit-like opening through which her tiny tongue went in and out like the tongue of a thirsty, hungry bird.

Once more I looked around. All the houses were closed, their lights out, the ground covered with black asphalt, not a single green leaf breaking its dark monotony. I searched the pavement for a morsel of bread but my hand came away with a handful of dust. I licked my skin, hoping to suck up a drop of water, but it was as dry as leather. The sharp, needling pain which I knew so well began to prick me below the breast. My hand started to feel my chest, slipped down over my breast and squeezed. My fingers surrounded my black nipple and began to squeeze, to pull, to pinch, but not a single drop of milk flowed out. They moved over to the other breast and began to squeeze so hard that they almost pulled it off my chest, but it was as dry and as hard as the udder of an old cow.

My other hand crept over to help and the ten fingers squeezed together but nothing came out. My fingers now were moving restlessly, greedily all over my body from one shoulder to the other, from my thighs to my belly, from my neck to my head, pressing and squeezing wherever they went. But my flesh was as dry and as sterile as desert sands which yield not a drop of water.

The tiny tongue was still dry, still moving in and out of the narrow slit, as though panting for breath. My fingers began to slide over my breast again, then down to my body, sparing no part of it. My nails dug into my flesh and each time came out without a single drop, as though all the fluids in my body, even the blood, had dried up. I sank my teeth into my flesh, but they came out holding nothing, spotlessly clean. I could see the marks left by nails and teeth in my flesh, like the bruises and long scratches which a whip can leave behind. My clothes were now in shreds, and my body was completely naked.

The tiny tongue continued to dart in and out with its panting movement. The air that came out with it was hot, as hot as my breath, and now it was my tongue that kept darting in and out with that strange rapid movement, with that same regular, unceasing rhythm as though it was my chest which continued to pant.

I do not think that you have ever had to pant. You are a medical doctor, practising a respected profession. You have a clinic which earns good money. I do not think that you can even imagine what it is like for a tongue to move in and out with this panting movement, especially if it is the tongue of a child. Your tongue would become dry and sharp as a knife. It would singe your throat like a tongue on fire, and your saliva would change into burning drops that fall into your stomach and pierce through it. I used to stand on the street, stark naked, my tongue hanging down over my chin and neck, my eyes bulging as though I were choked. I wanted to scream so that people would hear me. But all the windows were dark and shut. Behind them people lay asleep; I could almost hear them snoring. I wanted to bang on their doors with all my might, or gather stones and throw them at their windows. I wanted to wake them up so that I could tell them what I wanted.

I saw the tiny tongue stop its panting movement suddenly, I saw it hang down over the chin, over the slender neck. I saw the long, bulging artery pulsate with a regular movement. My finger crept over and felt the artery. My finger was icy cold, but the artery was hot. I could see its slow pulsations, but my finger was unable to feel them. I wanted to feel the throb that I had felt before, but I could not. I pressed down on the artery, but it fled from under my fingers so I pressed down on it more strongly.

Like a distant dream seen in my sleep years ago and forgotten, I was able to remember what was about to happen: the feeling of that artery still living under the tip of my fingers as I pressed and pressed, and it fled and fled, the blood starting to drain from my head, from my chest and my thighs, to collect in my finger, carrying with it all the energy and strength I needed. I could no longer feel the artery but I continued to press down on it. My head was cool, drained of its blood but not of its consciousness. I could understand, I could feel, I could see everything. I could see your small, white finger over my long, brown finger, pressing down until the artery turned white, until the small, smooth body had become white, until everything around was as white as a sheet. Yet it was an unusual whiteness, a whiteness that is not intrinsic in the thing itself, not a colour, but a whiteness which draws its source from the eye itself, like a white spot over the black pupil, or a white membrane over the retina in the depths . . .

★

Till then I had not understood that, like the body, thought must be born in pain. I imagined that ideas can be born without people feeling pain. Now I had discovered that suffering is a necessary thing, that thoughts which are not born in pain are not really living things, are like a piece of flesh, like an embryo in its mother's belly, guided by thoughts which are not its own, like the millions of particles moving in the air, on the land, in the sea, like gnats and fish and crocodiles and millions of people who have not known what suffering is.

My thoughts were still immature, still young. Yet they were able to take my tall, slender body to your clinic. I wanted to see you, and I wanted you to see me, to look into my eyes and realize that I had done my task. I was only a fine instrument in your hands, but I had succeeded in following the path you had set for me. I was eager to look into your eyes and see joy at my success. You were not in your clinic. I looked for your house but could not find it. So I went to my father's room. I knew I would find it empty, find his bed empty, find his coat which hung on the hook behind the door empty, and yet I stood in the middle of the room, gazing at his coat in amazement, as though it were only at this moment that I had noticed it was empty.

I went to my office at the newspaper. My desk was there, but it was not my old desk. It was a bigger desk with a glass top. On the desk I found a small book. On the cover was printed a name composed of only four letters. Perhaps I had seen the name before; I had often seen the book on my desk. In fact I used to see it every day, but my hand never picked it up; I did not feel a need to open it, to read it. I was not in the habit of reading anything. I hated words in print. They looked all the same to me, like the letters of my name in print at the end of my article, thrown at the bottom of the column like a brick.

That night my fingers reached out for the book. It was winter. Night had fallen and the offices of the newspaper were empty. I sat at my desk all alone. It was dark and I could not see the words clearly, so I put on the lamp. Its light fell over the pages, and for the first time I could see them and read them. I did not progress from one word to the other, for it was as though they did not form sentences to be read one following after the other. My eyes would fasten themselves on one of the sentences and an idea would pass through my head. As soon as I moved to another sentence, a different idea would occur to me. Thoughts kept going through my mind like rows of pinheads, or like the tiny feet of marching ants. There was nothing original or new about them. They were as old as the world itself: that human beings are born from their mothers' wombs, or that they die and are buried in the earth. Yet all these thoughts seemed wonderful and filled me with awe. But soon after would follow another sentence and everything would appear old and boring and already-known. The wonder would die away and even human beings, even life itself, would lose its freshness, its newness. I could feel an icy cold current creep down from the tip of his fingers to his pen, a dark cloud float in front of his eyes. But soon afterwards the cloud would disappear, and the warm elegance of his lines would shine through again. For a moment I felt relaxed, at ease, almost safe, then immediately afterwards my pulse quickened, my breathing grew more rapid as I tried to see through him, to anticipate what came next, and I found myself stealing a frightened glance at the line which came next.

There was magic, a secret magic in the way he arranged his words one after the other, so that no matter how ordinary they were, they seemed new. These words belonged to him alone, they were his, they served to create a language of his own. They were strange and yet familiar, knowable, understandable, so that one could almost detect them in the deepest part of oneself, for they were indeed the deepest part of that self.

For the first time my mother's face rose up before me. It was a rounded face with fair skin, and she had two round, blue eyes, as blue as the sea in Alexandria. Her breasts were full and in the centre of each breast she had something pointed, as dark as black liquorice. I used to hold it in my mouth and suck at it. A warm liquid would flow into my mouth and down inside me. It made my lids heavy, and so I would close my eyes and fall asleep.

The first time we met it was in winter. The rain pattered down on the window panes in my office. I had seen him before several times, but this time I raised my eyes from the desk, at the same time as he lifted his head to look at me, and our four eyes touched midway with nothing between them. The white of his eye touched the white of my eye, and his black pupil lay over the black of my pupil so that I could almost reach as far as the clear, blue depths of his eyes.

I opened my lips, preparing to say something, but his head had gone back to its usual position, poring over his papers. So I bent my head over my papers, but my letters on the sheet were now all crooked, just like they had been when I was a child. I put down one word after the other, but the sentences they formed on the paper had little meaning. The thoughts which lighted up in my mind quickly went out, once they touched the paper, and new ideas seemed to become worn out and as cold as the world itself. What if human beings were born from the wombs of mothers, and what if they were buried in a tomb? Ever since the beginning of the world, men and women had been born from the bellies of their mothers, and had died and been buried under the earth.

My eyes wandered to his long fingers as they curled around his pen and moved it over the paper with a slow regularity, like long, slow strides, one foot following the other with a slow deliberation, for each foot knew the distance it had covered with one step, and the distance it had to cover with the next. Each foot placed its full length on the right spot, pressed down on it with all its weight. When his pen moved over the paper I could almost hear the sound of steps, see my father's big feet treading by my side as we walked down the street to my school. My lips parted as though I were on the point of saying something, but I remained silent. I knew that my father had died many years ago, and that I would never see him again.

So I bent over my papers once more. I started to improve my handwriting, and to write the letters slowly as I used to do when I was a child, to go back over the words so that I could insert the commas and the full stops, dot the 'i's and cross the 't's. My fingers looked small and stumpy, yet before they had looked big and long, especially when at certain moments you used to put your hand on my wrist to feel my pulse. I used to feel ashamed at the sight of my long, brown fingers next to your small, white hand. I thought you could feel that my hand was rough so I used to draw it away quickly from under your hand.

No doubt you noticed this because each time you used to look me over carefully and examine me with an eager curiosity. You were capable of discovering things about me, and of understanding them easily. At times I used to hide things from you, and even lie to you. I did not want you to know these things, did not want you to examine me the way you did, and find out about me. At such moments I used to hate your eyes, hate your hands, hate your metal stethoscope, your sharp needle, and your thick eye-glasses. What is it that you were able to see deep down in me? I used to ask you, but like all doctors you did not answer. You would pull off your gloves, purse your lips, and scribble a prescription.

The pain was in my chest under the right breast. It pricked me like a needle, and your medicines did not cure me, your painkillers did not kill the pain, and your tranquillizers did not calm me. Nothing did anything to me. When I used to take hold of my pen the pain would shoot up to my right shoulder, then drop down to my arm and continue to the palm of my hand. The pen became heavy between my fingers, and left a deep impression.

I used to stretch out my fingers under your eyes, but you did not seem to notice anything. You would shake your head as though you did not care, and did not believe me. What kind of a human being are you? Have you never felt pain at all? Have you never known suffering? Or is it medical practice that is capable of turning people into stones? I walked out of your clinic that day with the intention of never returning. You do not know anything about my sickness. You do not feel my pain, nor do you know the simplest things about me.

I went to the newspaper where I worked. I had to go, sit at my desk, take hold of my pen, let the pen move over the paper. But the movement of my hand was not like his movement, was not slow, steady, regular. His words were like permanent markings lying on the paper, just as a big, heavy foot treading on mud leaves well-defined footprints when the mud has dried.

He did not use to lift his head from over the paper to look at me. He did not use to see me. I would be sitting on my chair with my upper half above the level of my desk, but he did not notice it. I thought he did not notice it because I was not in the habit of moving it. Perhaps he thought it was a statue, the bust of a woman sitting at her desk with a pen between her fingers. Or perhaps he thought it was an advertisement in the newspaper. I moved my hand over the paper but he did not lift his head. So I filled the paper with my writing, then folded it and put it in his hand.

You will never know this pain. You are a doctor, not a woman. The pain of that moment in which a woman finds herself in the presence of a man, unseen, unfelt. Her heart becomes like a short, pointed stone, tied to a string which sinks down into her belly. It might hook on to one or other of the organs of her belly but, whether it does nor not, it continues to rise and fall, to move here and there at the front, and at the back, but never settles in one place or stops its movement.

I wish you were a woman so that you would know! The pain was not how I described it. It was not like a pointed stone. It was the heart itself which was in pain, the heart with its flesh and blood, pulled here and there by the stone, strangled by the silk thread so that the pain was not only in the belly, but spread to every part of the body.

My office was on the second floor. I used to climb up a narrow spiral staircase to reach it. The stairs became narrow near the centre so that they were barely wide enough for the body of one person. On that day I had just put my foot on the first stair on my way down when I discovered that he had done the same thing also. Our bodies collided. The stairs seemed to grow darker and narrower as they spiralled down, so I pushed him aside slightly with my hand, and asked him about the folded paper I had given him. But he did not hear, or perhaps he did not speak. So I pushed him again with my hand. But he refused to answer, and shoved me away with his body. Where we stood it was very narrow and dark, and movement was barely possible, but I was able to move back slightly and look into his eyes. I could see the blue colour shining out from under the black, but he kept bending towards me, pulling back with his head all the time while I kept pushing his trunk backwards and trying to get our heads as close to one another as I could. He turned round with a quick movement so that now his bottom was hard up against me, while his head was on the other side. I thrust his bottom away with my hand as hard as I could and tried to get his head back where it would be close to mine, but each time his buttocks would spring back, and his head swing to the other side.

The staircase was dark and narrow so that our bodies kept whipping against one another like snakes in a fight, one of them after the tail and the other trying to get at the head. My foot slipped on the stairs, so I had to hold on to the railings to prevent myself from falling into the stairwell. Sometimes his foot would also slip, and he would fall down a few stairs before quickly pulling himself up to where I stood.

Our clothes were now all torn, and we were panting with exertion, but he insisted on giving me his backside whereas I was decided on his head. The darkness seemed to close in on us, and the staircase was narrow and suffocating, yet the battle went on. I was able to halt for a moment to take my breath, and in one flash, for the first time, I could see the whole scene. I was standing on one foot, toes holding on to the stair, my body swaying in the air, while he held on to the railings with one arm. I could see the dark, thick hair in his armpit. I suddenly remembered my father's naked body as I had seen it one night. The body of this man, exposed before my eyes like the masculinity of my father, laid bare before me, struck me as strange. This realization was like a split second of lucidity, of light, before our bodies, hidden in the dark once again, became locked in their struggle.

We went on. Each time our bodies collided on the staircase I refused to give in, and so did he. We continued to tear one another's clothes, to sweat and to gasp for breath, but we still went on. Now and again we would be surprised by feet going up or coming down from the newspaper offices and be obliged to make way quickly for whoever it was, as though we were total strangers and did not know one another. Once the sound of the steps had faded we rushed at one another again like fighting bulls. At one moment I glimpsed the chief editor in person climbing the stairs and stepped back quickly. My foot slipped on the stairs and I would have fallen onto his bald head had I not leapt up in time to hold on to the railings with both hands.

I doubt if you have ever known a determination of this sort. You are a doctor, not an artist. You have not been through that particular moment when an artist realizes that another artist does not feel his existence. Or when a writer in the presence of another writer finds out that his works are not read. At that moment all colours dissolve into one colour, into black. The desk, the walls, the papers, the fingers and the nails all become black. It is not the colour black to which our eyes are accustomed when we look at something black, such as black ink for example, but a strange black which we cannot detect unless our eyes are closed. This black is not really a colour, but rather a thick tissue which lines the inner surface of the eyelids, and prevents light, all light, from entering the eye.

Have you experienced this kind of panic? The kind of panic that seizes you when the electric light goes out and you feel for an instant that you have gone blind? It is not only a feeling of panic, it is something more, a terrible pain which makes you blind despite the fact that your eyes can see, or makes you feel you are able to see although in fact you are blind, so that the dividing line between seeing and not seeing, between sight and blindness, is not more than a fine hair, almost invisible and yet felt inside the eye cutting through the black pupil like a knife, and grazing the white eyeball with every rise and fall of the lid.

I almost walked into the door when I left the premises of the newspaper. Once in the street I huddled up against the wall, hurrying along the pavement. I was afraid of colliding with something. I found myself in front of your clinic. You pointed your torch into my eye, and there was the hair right in the centre of your lens, almost penetrating into your eye, and yet you could not see it. That day I lost faith in all your medicine.

For what has medicine taught you if it has not taught you these simple things? Were you not capable of catching hold of a small pair of tweezers and pulling out the hair, just as you pull out a lash that has fallen between the eye and the lid? Despite that, you were as overbearing as any doctor usually is. You washed your hands, closed your lips tight together, plugged your ears, and wrote the usual scribble on your piece of paper. Then, still wearing your white coat, you disappeared through the door.

I returned to the newspaper. My feet knew their

way, for there was no other way. That day, as usual, I sat at my desk, and as usual he sat behind his desk, panting. Suddenly his long fingers curled round my folded paper, but it was no longer folded. His eyes fastened themselves on my words for a long moment, long as the day. Suddenly he lifted his head. My head was already held upright. Our four eyes touched, with nothing to intervene between them, so that the white of his eye lay over the white of my eye, and the black of his eye over the black of my eye. I was able to penetrate through the black of his eyes to the layer of blue underneath, and on it I could see the letters of the words, shining. In less than a moment I was leaning on his desk, my shoulder against his shoulder, my breasts against his chest, my lips against his lips and my knees close up against his knees. I sat on his knees the way I used to do with my father when I was a child. I wanted him to move his knees like a see-saw just as my father used to do with me, so that I could sway in the air. But the eyes of our colleagues had started to follow what we were doing, and the desk was obstructing his knees, so he bent down under the desk and took me to him. The season was winter and the floor was covered with cold tiles. His body, enveloping mine, had a wonderful warm feeling. I curled around myself like a foetus so that he could envelop me with his body, and take me closer and closer to him.

I did not realize exactly what was happening. My

ability to feel was greater than my ability to understand, greater than my ability to express myself in words, greater than words themselves could express. I wish you were a woman, so that you could understand that moment when a man holds a woman in his arms, when the woman holds the man in her arms, when every part in each of them lies close up against the same part in the other, when there is such a perfect correspondence of these parts, that each one feels the totality and the detail of the other, their touching bodies leaving no space for anything to intervene between them, even a breath of air.

I do not think I was breathing. There was no air to breathe but I did not feel I was suffocating, or that I needed air. On the contrary, I longed to suffocate, longed to have my ribs squeezed even more closely so that my chest would be emptied of air, my belly emptied of air and every cell in my body emptied of its air bubbles. I could feel the air bubbles in my body and head, like small swellings exerting pressure on my flesh, on my nerves and blood vessels.

I was being squeezed. The small swellings inside me were being squeezed until they burst so that they disappeared one after the other in a curious way and with a wonderful regularity. They all disappeared completely, except for a single swelling, which has remained to this day, like a small abscess, or a small grain of corn carrying its seed inside it, filling up with water and air, swelling all the time, turning round and round but refusing to burst.

When I came out from the desk that day, the small swelling had not burst. He and I were still close to one another, and my fingers were still disengaging themselves from his. I looked at my fingers and they seemed to have become smaller, the skin on them more smooth, the tips tapering. I left the newspaper and rushed to your clinic. I wanted you to feel my pulse, to rest your hand on my hand so that your fingers would be over mine. That day when your fingers rested on mine I did not pull away my hand quickly as I had done the previous times. I hesitated and wilfully let it stay under your hand for a long moment. I wanted you to look at my fingers so that you would notice that they had become smooth and tapering, that they were now as smooth as your fingers were. But you did not notice them. You were busy looking at the hands of your watch and counting my pulse. Not one single time were you able to understand me, to know what was going on inside me. I used to tell you that deep inside there was something turning round, and would take your hand and hold it over the bare triangle where my stomach is. The spot under the tip of your finger was round as a grain, and kept revolving round itself like a hornet, but your finger could not feel it, or feel its movement.

At the beginning its movement was not violent. It was a slight movement and I would feel it in my belly, creeping lightly over the walls of my arteries, like a small, quiet wave. But after a while it began to sound like a pulse, and to beat exactly like a heart. Its beats were weak, soft, almost inaudible. I could not hear them in my ears but I would feel them under my palm like shivers, like a fine vibration which resembled warm water flowing quietly under the skin, or like the warm flow of blood in an artery.

I began to hear the beats, beat by beat. They would move from my belly to my chest, and from my chest to my neck, so that after a while I would hear the beats as though they were the beating of a pulse in my hand. When I put my hand on my belly I could feel the contours of the head, round and smooth, and I could almost catch hold of it but it would slip away from my fingers and disappear somewhere inside. I would hide my hand behind my back and wait. Then it would surface once more behind the walls of my belly, and I could feel the softness of it in my chest. I would bring my hand out cautiously from behind my back, and try to touch it with the tip of my finger, but it would shrink away like a porcupine and sink deep to the bottom.

It was as though we were playing a game. I would put my hand over my eyes to cover them, and hide my other hand under the bedcover, then hold my breath. As soon as everything was quiet she would begin to move in her hideout, stretch out a small, smooth arm to feel her way, then, when she felt safe, return to the surface and begin to play, jumping, and kicking the air with her hands and feet. I could feel her kicks on the wall of my belly, like small, velvet balls, knocking against it and bounding back.

My belly would rise and form a convexity in order to protect her. Whenever I stood up or sat down it would knock against the desk, so I would wind my arms under my belly, and almost carry it on my palms as I walked. In the street I would lift it up high so that people could see it and I could feel proud. In bed I would raise it up to my chest and nurse it.

I wish you were not a doctor. I wish you were my mother; then you would have known! You would have known the moment when you open your arms but instead of encircling empty air with them, you encircle something else, a small body smooth as your own belly, warm as your own breast. And in your breast the warm milk begins to flow and collect in your breast, and you feel it like small ants, or grains of fine sand, so soft and so fine that it sends a shiver through your depths.

A strange shiver kept going through my skin, in small shocks. I felt awe in my heart, a feeling which dropped down to my belly, made me bend over it, filled me with fear lest the sound of the pulse fade away, lest the velvet kicks cease all of a sudden, lest everything become still as a corpse. I bury myself in the blankets and shake. When I close my eyes I am unable to sleep, and the shaking in my body goes on. Then the small, smooth body begins to descend. I can feel its small, round head moving down over the bones of my back. I can almost see the fine, black hair through the wall of my belly. It continues to descend and I imagine it dropping out suddenly, but it does not. It remains wedged between the bones of my pelvis all night and refuses to budge.

So I fill my chest with air, hold it up, then press on it with both my hands to push it out. Sometimes I jump on my toes, trying to shake it down. When I go to the newspaper and sit behind my desk I feel as though it is lying wedged in between the bones of my thighs, so I stand up suddenly, thinking that it might drop out, but it remains where it is without moving an inch.

It did not cause me any pain. The bones of its head were round and soft. They pressed against my belly so gently that it was as if they did not press. Its long, smooth hair was like silver threads that touched my skin, and caused a soft current to go through my body to my chest, like the tiny legs of marching ants collecting over my breast. My fingers moved to my breast, encircled the nipple with their cold and trembling touch. At their tips hung the remnants of an old memory, like a distant dream, like the dry touch of a dry nipple pinched and squeezed and pressed between ten fingers, yet yielding not a single drop, like a dream I had seen in my sleep many years ago and forgotten. My heart was now beating like a drum, my chest was rising and falling, and my ten fingers were contracting over my nipple like wires of steel.

I do not think your mind can imagine what was happening to me at that moment. You are a doctor and you have no breast, so you cannot tell. My fingers were icy cold and suddenly something warm like blood dropped over my finger. It was not red like blood. It was white as light, a pure, luminous white, and it kept gushing out of the narrow opening like a fountain, and started to run down my arms like a river.

My body jumped to its feet and the next moment it was running down the street. I heard the sound of my heels on the asphalt road. They made a tapping sound, the same tapping sound which had echoed in my ears for long years and was linked to the day when I passed my final examinations and ran home to my father to give him my certificate. I looked into his black eyes, saw the layer of deep, transparent blue hiding in their depths like the surface of a lake. I knew that my father had died many years ago. I found myself standing in front of your clinic. I wanted to look into your eyes so that I could see my happiness reflected in them. When I saw the lights on I leapt up the steps with joy, and almost fell on my face. But as usual you stared at me with a stony look, then after a while you put your spectacles on. The small, round head with the small, black hair was wedged between the bones right under your eyes. It was not an eyelash lodged under the lid which might have escaped your attention. It was a whole head with bones and flesh and hair. Yet you were unable to see it. So I shrieked at you and began to squeeze the nipple of my breast with my fingers until a hot, white stream shot out into your eye. You took off your gloves, washed your hands, sucked your lips, and scribbled the usual stuff on your paper. A moment later you were on the verge of turning your back on me.

My arm stretched out and stopped you before you could turn. The palm of my hand rested on your neck. The long artery on your neck was beating, and my fingers were very cold. An old remembered dream clung to their tips, the feeling of a long artery which pulsates as they press down to blot it out. Everything suddenly turned white. Your neck became white, and your face became white, and your hair turned white, and your coat and your fingers and your nails were all coloured white. It was a different white, a strange white which arises not from the thing itself, a white which is not a colour, but a quality which comes from the eye as though a white spot has lain on the black pupil for years.

Until this moment I had not known that freedom, like the human body, must be born in pain. I thought that people were born free without feeling anything. But I learnt that pain is needed, that freedom, if not born in pain, is never born, that it remains an abstract thought throbbing in the mind, a child in its mother's womb which kicks but does not come out, a piece of flesh that moves as do millions of particles on the land, in the sea and air, millions of gnats and fish and crocodiles, and millions of people who have not known what freedom means.

My freedom was newborn like an infant baby, but it was capable of guiding my tall, slim body further along the way. I moved my arms and legs in the air as though I were moving them for the first time. I went to my office at the newspaper, sat at my desk, watched my long fingers curl around my pen, move over the paper slow and sure, like a firm tread, as a foot confident in itself takes one step after the other over a ground it knows well, measuring the length of its step behind, and the length of the step it will take in front, knowing exactly where to press down full length with its weight. I shifted from one word to the other, and each time my eyes rested on a sentence a thought would come to my mind, but as soon as they moved to the next sentence another thought would take its place. The thoughts succeeded one another in my mind like the march of many ants, like rows of needle heads, I could almost hear them moving on. They were not new thoughts. They were as old as life itself, that human beings are carried in their mothers' wombs and are born from their bellies, or that they die and are buried in the earth. Yet everything seemed extraordinary, a cause for wonder. Then a new sentence would come and the wonder would wear out. Even life would appear ordinary, an oft-repeated dream that keeps coming back. I could feel the tips of my fingers grow cold, see a haze before my eyes as though a white patch had grown over them. But soon the cloud which covered my eyes would disperse. A light started to shine out from the lines. For a short while I felt relaxed and confident, but soon afterwards my pulse became rapid, my breathing quick, and I tried to move ahead of time, to glimpse the words that were still to be born on the line.

It was as though some hidden magic lived inside the old familiar words so that when I arranged them one after the other on the line they were transformed into new words which I had never heard or read before. Words that belonged to me alone, that created a language for me alone, different sadnesses and different joys that were mine alone. They seemed strange to me and yet I knew them well. I could feel them all far away somewhere buried in my depths, with a throb like the throb of a heart, and a consistency soft and rounded like the surface of a liver.

My fingers moved to feel my heart but instead they curled round a small body, with a rounded head covered in silky hair and two black eyes which hid a transparent blue colour in their depths, shining like a mountain lake. I remembered my father's eyes when he used to look at me after I had succeeded in my examinations. My heart started to beat in the way it did when it was happy. I surrounded the small, soft body with my arms, my shoulders, my chest. I pressed it to me tighter and tighter but stopped the moment I noticed it had started to pant. I saw its tongue protruding, small and red and wet, like the tongue of a bird. My breast dropped out all by itself from the opening of my bodice, and the black nipple quivered in the air. On its furrowed, black skin something like an old dream seemed to cling, something like the feel of a small, dry tongue, tiny jaws without teeth, then soft gums biting and biting. The nipple slipped into the little mouth, and two small jaws closed their soft gums on it.

I felt something warm and soft flow from the back of my head to my nipple then into the small mouth, like a thin stream of hot blood flowing through a long artery.

My lids became heavy then dropped down over my eyes. I felt I was falling asleep, or losing consciousness. Until that moment I had not known that extreme pleasure and extreme pain have something in common, that they are both difficult to bear and may cause one to lose consciousness.

But I did not lose consciousness. I was in full possession of my senses, and could feel the small, soft body resting on my chest. It had begun to close its lids with satisfaction, and its jaws released their hold on my nipple, as though it were falling asleep.

I watched the little features as they relaxed and yielded to sleep. They were very familiar to me. I had seen them hundreds or even thousands of times before, in the mirror, in the photographs on the wall and in particular the photograph which hung in my bedroom, showing me as a child lying on my belly in bed.

Was I being born a second time, beginning it all over again, like a bail of thread that had rolled round and round until it was empty, then been filled up on the spinning wheel so that it could begin rolling out again?

My finger stretched out, trying to reassure itself with the feel of the small body. Five tiny fingers curled around it like a thread of silk. Small, dark fingers, the colour of my fingers, the nails shaped like mine. Yet my fingers were big and coarse, the bones of my arms and legs looked huge, like the bones of a strange old woman.

Till then I had not discovered where this child had come from. It was not an ordinary child, for all children had a father. I did not know its father, and I did not try to find out. Even if I had tried, it was not possible for me to discover who the father was. All I knew was that I was the mother, and that I fed it and satisfied its needs.

The child also satisfied my need. When I looked into his big, black eyes I could see the blue colour shining through from the depths like a lake, so I almost never felt the bite of hunger or the need for sleep.

I would hold him tight in my arms, resting on my chest. I was afraid to sleep then wake up in the morning to find he had disappeared. If my lids dropped over my eyes I wrapped my arms around him. When I felt his body in my arms it seemed like a dream. I feared that when I opened my eyes everything would have vanished into thin air.

I never left him alone. I carried him in my bag whenever I went somewhere. At the newspaper I hid him in the bag and put the bag in the drawer. Every now and then I opened the drawer, then the bag, to look into his eyes, and when the shining blue colour looked out from the depths of his black eyes I would laugh at the top of my voice.

No one realized why I was laughing. I stifled the sound of my laughter so that when it burst out it was soundless. I was afraid somebody would hear me laughing and would try to find out why, to search my things, open my drawer and find the bag hidden inside.

The drawer had a lock, and the bag had a key which I used to hide in the deep cleft between my breasts. Yet I was afraid that someone might watch me and find out where I hid it. Opposite me there were eyes that followed me closely, and one day they saw me when I took the key out of the opening of my bodice, so I carried the bag away in my arms and went out to look for another place which would be safer.

Some distance away I opened the bag and he came out, walking on his own two legs. The air was cold so I took off my jacket and wrapped him up inside its folds, all the while holding his small fingers in my hand. But he kept pulling his fingers away from mine trying to extract them from my grasp and run away. I ran after him. I was afraid to let him cross the road on his own. He was still a small child and I could see his small, thin body in the middle of the street which was crowded with people and cars. He looked like a white spot in a dark, stormy sea. He never stopped moving and jumping away from me. I followed behind so that I could catch up with him and hold him in my arms. He kept avoiding my hold, slipping out of my arms, trying to run away from me but I did not give him a chance. I followed him like a shadow, as though I were a part of his body, like his hand, or his arm, or his head. One day he hit his head against the wall trying to get rid of the weight of my body. I was stronger than a wall. When my fingers reached out for him and caught him, they would grasp the little hand tightly, almost in a stranglehold, like a silken thread winding itself around him. I would watch him as he tried to extract the fingers of his hand one by one from my grasp, but each time he freed one finger the silk thread would twine itself around it like a spider's web. One day he sank his teeth into my hand, but my hand did not let go. I was afraid to let him free lest he slip far away into the crowded street and be run over by a car, or swallowed up in the seething crowds which resembled a stormy sea.

At night I never slept except with my fingers curled around his hand, and I always waited for him to fall asleep. I was afraid to fall asleep before he did. My fingers could lose their grip and he might succeed in slipping away.

I used to feed him during the day, and watch him grow at night. Every morning I awoke to find his arms and legs longer and heavier. His fingers grew longer than mine, his hands bigger than mine. He was now taller than I was. I wanted him to remain small and light so that I could carry him hidden in my arms. I wanted his fingers to remain small and thin so that I could curl my fingers around them, but my clasp could no longer fold around his hand and so he was able to escape from me. I ran after him. I ran as fast as I could, but his pace was faster than mine, and his legs were longer and more supple than mine. The distance between us began to grow so I tried to run faster and I started to pant. The street was crowded with people and with cars, and I could see him from the back and differentiate between him and others by the quick way in which he walked, by the small, red ears and the black beauty spot on the back of his neck. He was running without paying attention to the cars, and every time I heard the screech of brakes I shrieked, 'My child!'

Little by little I was becoming unable to see the street as clearly as I could see it before. It was as though the sun were setting, or as though a thin mist were settling before my eyes. I could no longer see his back, or his ears, but the black beauty spot continued its up and down movement before my eyes until it too became so distant that I could no longer see it.

The backs of the people in the street mingled so densely that I could no longer distinguish his back from the others'. My foot hit on a small stone and I fell down. I thought I would be able to get up quickly as I had always done and start running again, but the movement of my legs had become heavy and slow. The bones in my spine made a grinding sound over one another as though something was being milled between them.

I did not stop. I was afraid to stop. If I did I would never catch up with him again, and would lose him for ever. I bent over to prevent my bones from grinding against one another, and threw the weight of my body on my thighs and legs.

The bones of my thighs and legs started to give way under their heavy weight. I bought a thick stick and started to lean on it instead of letting my full weight come down on my feet. I could no longer see the backs of people, but a dim light kept falling over my lids and it helped me to find my way. I shuffled each foot behind the stick slowly. The stick hit against something hard and fell out of my hand. I could not remain standing on one leg so I sat down. I thought I would be able to pick up the stick, and stand up again as I had been able to do before, but I was not able to put my weight on the other leg and remained sitting where I was. I continued to follow the road, trying to penetrate through the deep haze with my eyes. At one moment it seemed as though the haze lifted, and I was able to discern a back which looked like that of my child. I knew it from the red ears, and the black beauty spot on the neck. I leapt to my feet, only to fall down on the ground again. I heard the bones of my skull hit the pavement.

My body now lay prone, my back on the tarmac road. The cold seeped through to my back but my face looked up and I could see the sky. Its blue colour dropped on my lids like a warm ray of light.

I was able to lift my lids from over my eyes for a short instant. The blue I saw was not the blue of the sky. In front of me I glimpsed the big, black eyes with that blue transparent colour lying in their depths like a lake. I tried to open my lips so that I could laugh out loudly, but my lips refused to part. I tried to stretch out my arm and wrap it round my child so that I could hold him to me, but my arm would not move. Through the thick haze I could see him crawl close up to me. I could feel the hot breath over my eyelids, and the long, smooth fingers slip over my face, feeling their way around my neck like a thread of silk. The mist in front of my eyes grew thicker and thicker like a fog, and the fingers enlaced themselves around my neck like a thread that kept pulling harder until it was fully stretched.

The blue colour disappeared very slowly and suddenly, all the things around me turned white, completely white, like a sheet of paper on which nothing is written. A sharp, shrill sound like that of birds singing rose in the air.

DATE DUE

GAYLORD   PRINTED IN U.S.A.